still awake

(a lily dawn fbi suspense thriller—book 3)

ava strong

Ava Strong

Ava Strong is author of the REMI LAURENT mystery series, comprising six books (and counting); of the ILSE BECK mystery series, comprising seven books (and counting); of the STELLA FALL psychological suspense thriller series, comprising six books (and counting); of the DAKOTA STEELE FBI suspense thriller series, comprising six books (and counting); and of the LILY DAWN suspense thriller series, comprising five books (and counting).

An avid reader and lifelong fan of the mystery and thriller genres, Ava loves to hear from you, so please feel free to visit www.avastrongauthor.com to learn more and stay in touch.

ISBN: 978-1-0943-3059-4

BOOKS BY AVA STRONG

LILY DAWN FBI SUSPENSE THRILLER
STILL ALIVE (Book #1)
STILL HOPE (Book #2)
STILL AWAKE (Book #3)
STILL HERE (Book #4)
STILL MAD (Book #5)

REMI LAURENT FBI SUSPENSE THRILLER
THE DEATH CODE (Book #1)
THE MURDER CODE (Book #2)
THE MALICE CODE (Book #3)
THE VENGEANCE CODE (Book #4)
THE DECEPTION CODE (Book #5)
THE SEDUCTION CODE (Book #6)

ILSE BECK FBI SUSPENSE THRILLER
NOT LIKE US (Book #1)
NOT LIKE HE SEEMED (Book #2)
NOT LIKE YESTERDAY (Book #3)
NOT LIKE THIS (Book #4)
NOT LIKE SHE THOUGHT (Book #5)
NOT LIKE BEFORE (Book #6)
NOT LIKE NORMAL (Book #7)

STELLA FALL PSYCHOLOGICAL SUSPENSE THRILLER
HIS OTHER WIFE (Book #1)
HIS OTHER LIE (Book #2)
HIS OTHER SECRET (Book #3)
HIS OTHER MISTRESS (Book #4)
HIS OTHER LIFE (Book #5)
HIS OTHER TRUTH (Book #6)

DAKOTA STEELE FBI SUSPENSE THRILLER
WITHOUT MERCY (Book #1)
WITHOUT REMORSE (Book #2)
WITHOUT A PAST (Book #3)
WITHOUT PITY (Book #4)
WITHOUT HOPE (Book #5)

PROLOGUE

Mikael sighed as he made his way through the resort restaurant, his feet clacking against the tile. It was a beautiful place to work. The restaurant was colorful, each table with its own vase of tropical flowers. The chairs were bright white and the walls a cool blue. The view was panoramic of the resort and the surrounding area. The long buffet table was lined with delectable dishes for guests to choose from.

Mikael wore a business suit, matching tie, and polished shoes. He looked like a businessman going out to lunch, and that was what the owners wanted—for the servers to look their best. But Mikael rarely got to enjoy the food here; the truth was, he couldn't afford it.

He was simply a waiter. And if he was lucky, he'd get some good tips.

The smells were appetizing and enticing to the nose: roast beef, potatoes, roasted root vegetables, and fancy breads. You could stay here all day and not get bored, and that was what some customers did.

As Mikael swiftly walked over to the bar to grab table eight its drinks, he glanced toward the outdoor patio, where a woman had been sitting since before his shift started, looking over the beach, a half-full margarita on the table.

Mikael had yet to serve her, as it seemed she was waiting for someone. She was still there now, but it was impossible to tell if she was enjoying herself or just… waiting. Maybe she'd been stood up?

Mikael was eager to finish his shift and head back to his condo, where he could sit on his couch and watch television while he waited for his girlfriend, Renee, to come home. She worked at the resort's front desk, and he knew she would be working overtime tonight.

He was surprised by how much he enjoyed working at the resort. He was treated well by the management. He also enjoyed his coworkers, who were usually fun people, or they were at least fun to watch. He had a good view of the happenings at the resort and perhaps this was the reason he liked working there. Plus, the clientele were rich and tips were good—not enough to pay off the student debt for the degree he was never going to use, but he was working his way up. It was paradise, a resort based in a small, touristy community just north of West Palm Beach. It was quieter than other resorts, but it brought in the richer folks.

As he put another order in with the bar, he glanced back outside, and the woman was still sitting on the patio. One of his coworkers, Trisha, breezed past him, and he gently grabbed her arm.

"Hey, Trish, is anyone serving that woman over there?"

Trish looked out at the patio. The woman wore a sundress and a sunhat, but from this angle, they could only see the back of her.

"No idea," Trish said. "She's been there for a while."

"Hm. I'm gonna go check on her," Mikael said.

Mikael slowly made his way outside and approached the woman's table. He cleared his throat, but she didn't flinch. Her gaze, hidden beneath a large pair of sunglasses, was still fixed on the horizon as if she was expecting someone. And the ocean was beautiful right now, sparkling against the cerulean sky, and the Florida sun was hot and warm—maybe she'd fallen asleep?

"Good afternoon," Mikael said gently. "Can I get you anything?"

The woman remained silent. She seemed miles away in thought, lost in her own world.

"Hello, ma'am?" Mikael asked. "I know you aren't finished with your drink, but it's completely melted now… can I get you another?"

Still no response. He moved a little bit closer and could see her face now—she had large sunglasses on and she wasn't moving. He tried again, but still nothing.

Mikael was worried; he didn't know what to do in this situation. Was she okay? Should he call someone? He tentatively reached out and touched her arm gently, but there was no response or movement from her body.

He quickly pulled his hand back, because it was then that he noticed that something wasn't right—her skin felt cold and clammy to the touch. What the hell? It was hot outside and she was right in the sun… Mikael's stomach turned. This wasn't right.

"Ma'am," he said, too afraid to touch her again. "Are… are you okay?"

Just then, a seagull squawked and swooped down toward them. Mikael tried to wave it away, but the bird reached down—and snatched the sunglasses right off the woman's face with its feet.

And what Mikael saw made his blood run cold.

The woman's eyes were wide open and lifeless, staring out at the ocean. Not blinking. Not moving.

No…

She was dead.

CHAPTER ONE

Agent Lily Dawn of the FBI hadn't stepped foot on her home island of Aruba in years.

As she got off the boat, it was like something out of a dream. The white sand beaches stretched for miles, the crystal blue waters of the Caribbean Sea glistening in the sun. The colorful buildings that lined the shoreline sparkled with a hint of magic, and the air was filled with a tropical concoction of fragrances—sweet sea salt, fresh coconut, and blooming hibiscus. As Lily stepped off the boat, she breathed in the salty sea air and then tasted it on her tongue—a flavor that was unique to Aruba, a flavor that could only be found here on her home island.

She was really doing this. She was here.

Her nerves clenched inside her stomach as, carrying her small luggage bag, she made her way toward the beach, where she knew the exact route to take to her parents' place. Lily hopped off the dock, and her feet sank into the sand. She was surrounded by other people arriving at the island, and the number of bodies disoriented her, so she pushed on—homebound.

Home…

This place hadn't been her home in so many years. But now she was here again.

When she looked up at the houses that began past the beach, her heart nearly stopped.

Standing on the street, waiting for her, were her parents.

Her dad waved, and her mom stood with her arms tucked around her waist.

Lily couldn't believe it.

Her parents… despite the bad blood between them, despite how many years it had been, had still come to greet her.

It had been over ten years since Lily had taken her younger sister, Kara, to a party with her, right here in Aruba. That night, Lily had gotten drunk and fallen asleep next to a boy on the beach.

In the morning, Kara was gone.

She was never seen again.

The police never found her, or her body, and she had been declared "legally dead" about a year ago. Lily didn't believe that—it was very possible Kara was still out there somewhere…

Lily had done so much to atone for what she'd done. She'd become an FBI agent. She'd helped save countless people. But nothing would ever erase the fact that Kara had disappeared under her supervision. Lily would always blame herself.

She didn't blame her parents for blaming her, either.

But recently, Lily had reached out to her parents again and discovered that her father's health was declining. She told them that she needed to come see them. But Lily still hadn't spoken to her mother.

As Lily approached them, her heart thrummed with nerves. She was a mix of her parents' genetics, with her dad's Dominican tanned skin and her mother's Dutch blue eyes and blonde hair. The closer she got, the more she realized that her parents looked older now; her mother with more lines on her face, her father frailer and thinner than his once hearty self.

But Lily was still nervous to see her parents. She'd left them nearly a decade ago, when she'd been eighteen years old. And even though she'd tried to keep in touch over the years, this was the first time she'd seen them since then. So Lily wasn't sure how her parents would react to seeing her.

Lily reached them, and she saw that in their eyes were unshed tears. Her mother even had a hand over her mouth. The look of shock on her face was almost unbearable.

"Lily," her mother said, her voice trembling. She opened her arms.

Lily's jaw dropped. After all this time, her mother wanted to hug her?

Lily dropped her luggage and opened her arms to embrace her mother. As they hugged, Lily could feel her mom's body stiffen. She knew that her mother wasn't doing so well either. Their relationship wasn't the best, but Lily knew that if she didn't at least try to reach out to her, she'd regret it for the rest of her life.

There was something so foreign, and yet so familiar, about hugging her mom again after all these years. As the moment dragged on, each of them held the other tighter. Lily wished she could know what her mom was really thinking. When she pulled away, her mother coldly turned from her, which made Lily's heart sink.

But they had still hugged. It was progress.

Her dad was next, wrapping Lily in a big hug and holding her tight. "I missed you so much, *mija*."

Mija. It had been so long since Lily had heard the Spanish term for "my daughter" from her father's mouth, and it made her heart swell.

They let go of each other, and it seemed as if Lily's mom was about to say something, but then she turned away from them, walking toward their house.

"I need to lie down," her mother said, her back to them. She was clearly upset about something, but Lily didn't know what. Probably her being there. Either way, her mom took off up the street, getting a good head start on them.

Her father glanced at Lily.

They were alone.

Lily let out a deep sigh. She picked up her luggage and walked with her father up the street.

"Your mother is very upset," he said. "She has been… very upset for a long time."

Lily didn't say anything. What could she say? This was all her fault.

"But you're home now. And that's good," her father said.

Lily walked side by side with her father, their steps in sync as they made their way back home. She kept her gaze ahead, giving him a tight smile. The streets of Aruba were familiar to her; sunbaked sidewalks, stores painted in bright pastels, and the scent of salt in the air. A hint of lime wafted past as they walked, making Lily's mouth water and reminding her of Caribbean summers.

Soon, they reached the house. Lily's childhood home—the place she had grown up, spent all her formative years with her parents and sister here in Aruba.

It was a small, bright yellow, two-story building with a welcoming front porch. The windows were framed with white shutters, and the roof was covered in a blanket of red clay tiles. Inside the house, warm sunlight cascaded in through the windows and cast a comforting glow throughout the space. The walls were painted in soft shades of blue and green. There was a deep sense of nostalgia as Lily stepped through the door; she remembered moments shared with her family here: laughter, joy, games, celebrations. She felt at home here, in her childhood sanctuary.

She'd spent the best days of her life sitting on the beach just outside the house.

This home had once been her world.

But now, everything was different. And she had once been a child, but now, she was an adult. No, this wasn't her sanctuary anymore; this was a different place now, a place that had grown and evolved without her.

"You have time off work?" her father asked, going toward the kitchen.

"Yeah, should be a few days," Lily said. "I could get called back in any time, of course, but… I had to come make the visit."

"You did. We are glad to see you."

Her father went to the kitchen and grabbed a few bottles of water. He handed one to Lily, who took it and gulped down the cool liquid.

"I'm glad to see you, too, Dad," Lily said.

As they sipped their water, her dad looked out the kitchen window and stared out at the beach.

"A lot has changed since you've been gone," he said.

"Yeah," Lily said. "I know."

Her father turned to face her. "We have changed."

"I've changed, too," Lily said, glancing down at the ground.

"I'm glad you have," her dad said, a smile forming on his face. "You became a woman, a strong one. I'm proud of you."

Lily felt her eyes well up. "I'm sorry, Dad."

"You have nothing to apologize for," her dad said, a hint of sadness in his voice. "I'm sorry for how we treated you… like that."

Lily nodded. She knew her father was referring to how her parents had blamed her for Kara's disappearance. "I'm here now," Lily said, waving a hand at their surroundings.

"I know you two were never close," her father said. "But… you know your mother still loves you, right?"

Lily didn't want to talk about it. "I know. She'll get there… she just needs time."

Lily smiled, but she still felt guilty. Maybe her father was glad she was here. Maybe her mother would get there. Maybe everything would be alright. But Lily had already made up her mind.

Despite whatever her parents thought of her, she had to try and find Kara.

No matter what.

"Maybe I should go unpack?" Lily asked.

Her dad nodded. "Go ahead. We have your old bedroom upstairs, ready for you."

Lily smiled. "Thanks, Dad. I really appreciate it."

"I want you to be comfortable," her father said. "This is your home."

Lily picked up her suitcase and headed up the stairs. She opened the door to her room, and the moment she stepped inside, a wave of nostalgia hit her. It was the room she'd grown up in, the place where she had spent her childhood.

Her old, teal-colored bed was still there, the comforter and pillows simple, yet homey in design. Her old bookshelf was in the corner, filled with books she'd read long ago. She'd even left a few stuffed animals behind.

They were all here, as if waiting for her.

Lily placed her suitcase on the bed and sat down next to it. She looked around, smiling at the memories.

But then… she remembered Kara. And that smile quickly dropped from her face.

She opened her suitcase and grabbed the small, white frame with the photo inside it. Kara's face beamed out at her, and she could still feel her sister's soft, warm skin against her own.

"I'll find you, Kara," she whispered softly. "I promise you I'll find you."

She put the frame on the bedside table and dug through her suitcase. She took out a few things, then left the room, closing the door behind her.

Her parents' bedroom door at the end of the hall was closed, and Lily could infer her mother was in there, hiding. Lily sighed. She wished her mom would talk, but she knew she would when she was ready.

Lily glanced at the door to Kara's room as she walked down the hallway.

She hadn't been in there in so long. She wondered if they'd changed it, or if it was still the same.

Taking a breath, Lily went inside Kara's room.

Everything was the same. The bed was still there, covered with the same yellow comforter. The walls were painted a light shade of blue, and the room's centerpiece was a tall, wooden bookshelf filled with books.

She walked up to the shelf and ran her fingers over the empty space where her sister's toys had been. Kara would never have been able to leave her stuffed animals behind. If she'd been here, she would have taken them with her.

Lily turned around, looking at the bed. Her sister's favorite stuffed animals had always been on the headboard, but they were gone now.

Lily walked over to the bed and sat down. She remembered what it was like to lie here with Kara, and it brought a small smile to her face. But then, tears welled up in her eyes. It was hard to believe that it was really Kara's room. It was as if Lily had been transported back in time to when she'd spent her childhood in this house.

But Lily couldn't stay here for long. Her parents probably wouldn't like her sitting around in Kara's room, so she stood up to leave.

But as she did, a floorboard creaked beneath her foot in a way she'd never noticed before. What the…?

Lily had been in this room a million times since she was a kid. After Kara left, she spent a lot of time in here too, but she'd never noticed this floorboard. Lily looked down and saw there was a crack in it—as if it could be lifted.

Curious, Lily bent down and gave the floorboard a gentle tug. It lifted easily, revealing a secret cache of books beneath it. Her eyes widened as she saw them—occult books, in all shapes and sizes, with titles like *The Secrets of Black Magic* and *The Art of Alchemy*.

Lily had no idea where they'd come from, but this was definitely not what she expected to find under the floorboard. She grabbed one of the books and opened it up. It was filled with strange symbols and curious drawings that she hadn't seen before.

She looked around the room again, feeling Kara's presence more strongly than ever. What the hell was all this? Occult stuff, witchcraft, alchemy?

Lily thought she knew her sister pretty well, but she had never heard Kara show any interest in any of these topics. Why were they hiding under her floorboard?

Lily's phone buzzed in her pocket and startled her, causing her to drop the books. From downstairs, her father called up, "Lily, is everything okay?"

"Fine, Dad!" Lily didn't know how to handle this right now—she instinctively put the books back in the floorboard, thinking she'd deal with them later, and hurried into the hallway so she wouldn't get caught.

Her phone was still ringing. Going back to her room, she answered it.

Naturally, it was work.

"This is Agent Dawn," she said, trying to compose herself.

"Agent Dawn, it's Chief Aboye," said the chief, and Lily's heart fell. No—not now. She'd just gotten here…

"What is it, Chief?" Lily dared to ask.

"I know I said you could have a few days off to get situated in Miami, but we have another case, and I need you down at HQ ASAP."

Lily's heart sank. "Chief, I… I'm in Aruba."

"Aruba?" she said. "Are you visiting family?"

"I am. I only just arrived."

The chief sighed. "Agent Dawn…"

Lily quickly realized how this looked. Lily had only just been transferred to Miami, and this would be her third assignment—she couldn't skip it, even if she was in Switzerland.

"I'll be there, Chief," she said. "I'll take a private plane back to Miami, but it's going to take me a few hours."

"That's fine," the chief said. "Just get here. I'll let Agent Jackson know."

"Okay," Lily said. "I'll see you soon."

She hung up and let out a deep sigh. This was not how she wanted to start her new job. But there was nothing she could do about it. Not now.

She'd just have to explain to her parents that she'd be back as soon as possible… if they'd still have her.

CHAPTER TWO

As Lily walked into the FBI headquarters in Miami, she felt exhausted. She'd paid a local pilot to fly her down, but it had still taken forever, and she'd been buzzing with anxiety the whole time.

Her dad wasn't happy she was leaving so soon, but Lily left all her belongings in the room to show them she had every intention of coming back. Her father understood that her job as an FBI agent was demanding. Meanwhile, her mother told her she'd jumped the gun by thinking she'd have enough time off to come here, and should've booked a legitimate vacation.

Maybe that was true, but Lily had been too eager to see her parents. Miami was a lot closer to Aruba than Quantico, where Lily lived before, was, so she reminded herself that it would all work out.

It was late afternoon now as Lily took the elevator up to the right floor. She passed by her partner, Xander Jackson's, office, then found her way to Chief Aboye's.

Lily knocked, then entered. Chief Aboye was sitting across from Xander, who shot Lily a grin.

"Nice of you to finally join us, Lils," Xander said cheekily in his southern drawl. Lily tried not to roll her eyes. Xander had warmed up to her a bit since they'd started working together, and he wasn't bad looking either, but he still had a knack for getting under her skin. She'd take the nickname "Lils" over "sweetheart" any day, though.

"I'm so sorry I'm late," Lily said, taking a spot beside Xander and focusing on Chief Aboye.

"Not a problem, Agent Dawn," Aboye said. "You thought you had time off, and it was very last minute."

"That's not an excuse, ma'am," Lily said. "I apologize."

"Well, I don't think you need to apologize—you said you'd take an early flight back, and you're here now." Aboye paused, then she continued. "But now that you're here, I have an assignment for you."

An assignment… Lily felt a pang of guilt. She hadn't even unpacked her luggage back home, and here she was, sent on another assignment. But that was the life of an FBI agent—it was the risk she had to take. Having a personal life would always be hard, and work always had to come first.

"This one is turning out to be very odd," the chief said. She opened up a file and slid two photos across her desk, which Xander and Lily both leaned forward to view.

Each photo contained a Caucasian woman sitting on a chair, wearing a sun hat. And though there were no visible wounds, Lily knew a dead body when she saw one. There was no life in the women's eyes, and their skin was nearly blue.

"We have two victims so far," Aboye said. "Both of them were found staged like this at different resorts, only they had sunglasses on. In both instances, witnesses had removed the sunglasses, so they aren't seen in the pictures here."

Lily didn't know what to say. "The killer is staging the women to look alive and leaving them at resorts?"

"Yes," the chief said. "The killer is very careful—no one saw any of this, somehow."

"Does it seem like the victims knew each other? Shared the same social circles?"

"We're looking into it," Aboye said. "But so far, we haven't found any connection between the two women. They were found at very different resorts. One was found earlier today, the other three days ago."

Lily looked through the photos again. The tropical resort setting didn't make sense either. "Why would this killer go to all this trouble to preserve the victims, then leave them at a tropical resort?"

"Because he's a sadistic psychopath," Xander said, and he and Lily both looked at each other, then back to Aboye.

"That's what we've been thinking too," Aboye said, nodding. "But we haven't been able to come up with any profile that fits. No connection between the victims has been found. They don't seem to know each other, and they're from completely different walks of life." She pointed a dark finger at the first victim, a blonde. "This is Grace Maloney, twenty-nine. Wealthy, but self-made—a social media influencer who came from nothing. Then"—she pointed to the second victim, a brunette—"we have Veronica Smith, twenty-one, the daughter of very wealthy parents."

"So they're both rich, but not the same kinda rich," Xander said.

Chief Aboye nodded. “That’s right. We know Grace’s cause of death was asphyxiation, but Veronica’s has not yet been determined. The rest of the information on the victims is in their files, which you can review once you get going. We have a helicopter set up to take you down to Ashlyn—it’s a community just north of West Palm Beach, and that’s where the resort Veronica was found in is located.”

Lily nodded again and scooped up the files from the chief’s desk.

“And you two,” the chief said. “This thing—it’s really bad for tourism over there. I need you two on your absolute A-game. Got it?”

“Yes, Chief,” Lily and Xander said together.

She’d been on enough of these cases to know that a lot of work was ahead of her and her partner, and they’d need to be at the top of their game.

“No slip-ups,” the chief said. “I want to see this thing solved.”

“We can do that,” Lily said. “And, ma’am… I’m grateful for the opportunity.”

Aboye smiled. “Thank you, Agent Dawn.” She gave Xander a look. “And you too, Jackson. I’m trusting you two to get this done in record time.”

They nodded, got up, and left the room, reconvening in the hallway. Side by side, Lily walked with Xander, clutching the victims’ files.

“You ready for round three, Dawn?” Xander asked, shooting her a coy grin as they approached the elevator.

But Lily was antsy as they got inside. Antsy to solve the crime, and antsy to get it over with ASAP so she could get back to Aruba.

“I really need us to focus on this one,” Lily said. “I don’t want to lose any more girls.”

“We’re a dream team, aren’t we?” Xander shot her another grin. “I’m not worried about it. We’ll hash it out. But you seem like you’re in a rush. Something you wanna tell me?”

Lily glanced up at him. As much as he annoyed her at times, Xander was still her partner, and he had a right to know.

“I was late because I was visiting my parents in Aruba,” Lily said. “I need to get back there as soon as I can.”

Xander nodded. “I get it. I’ve got family too, not that I ever wanna see them again.” He paused, then he continued, “I’m sure they miss you.”

Lily felt a pang in her chest. She missed her parents too, and she was anxious to see them again. “Yeah.”

The elevator doors opened, and as they stepped off, Lily's heart clenched in her chest. She just hoped they could solve this before another girl had to die.

CHAPTER THREE

The helicopter descended toward the remote beach, and Lily looked down at the white sand below as the rotary blades spun loudly above. It was late afternoon, and Lily felt like she'd already done two weeks' worth of traveling in just one day—but it was only just beginning.

Ashlyn was a small, but wealthy community just north of West Palm Beach, and it was more private and less traveled—Lily could tell, as this part of the beach was devoid of tourists. But up the coastline, she could see a yard of yachts and what appeared to be a massive resort.

Beside her, Xander was also looking out at the view, and in the front, their two pilots navigated the helicopter until it finally touched down on the sand.

"Welcome to Ashlyn Beach," the pilot said, then he turned around and smiled at them. "We'll be here for you if you need us, but we'll be at the dock. Just let us know."

Lily and Xander nodded, then they opened the door and stepped out into the hot Florida sun. Lily pulled out her aviator shades, and they both strode to the shore.

"Wow," Xander said. "This place is beautiful."

Lily nodded, and she couldn't help but agree with him. They'd arrived in the late afternoon, and the sun was beginning to set over the ocean, which was glimmering a deep, rich blue. The sand was white, like it had been painted that way, and in the sand, Lily saw some starfish and sea urchin shells. The water looked so clear and so… blue.

The setting was idyllic and peaceful. The warm, salty air down here felt so different from up in the sky, so much calmer. Lily took a deep breath, feeling a little bit more relaxed. For a brief moment, she could almost feel like she was back in Aruba—but she quickly rinsed that thought away.

This was no vacation. This was serious—someone had died here, and it was their job as FBI agents to get to the bottom of it.

Lily glanced over at Xander, and he nodded. He seemed to understand that this was no time for sightseeing, so they set off down the beach.

Lily and Xander began to make their way up the shoreline, toward the resort. As they got closer, it seemed bigger and more luxurious than it had looked from above. There were several buildings, all with immaculate white walls, and a large pool in the center of them all.

"Looks like they're doing well," Xander said as they approached.

Lily nodded, then stopped walking. In front of them was a police barrier that surrounded the entrance to the resort—this was where the victim had been found. Lily took another deep breath and reminded herself that this was what she'd signed up for—to help those who couldn't help themselves.

She stepped forward and flashed her badge at one of the officers guarding the entrance. He nodded at her, then waved them through without a word.

The resort was breathtaking. The buildings were mostly white and blue, with lush gardens and cascading waterfalls surrounding each building. It looked like a paradise; Lily almost wished she could stay here and forget about all the troubles of life.

But there was still work to be done, so she followed Xander up the steps toward the main entrance. As they walked in, their eyes adjusted to the dim lighting inside—and immediately, Lily could tell why this place was so popular among tourists.

The lobby was open and airy, with high ceilings and marble flooring lined with ornate rugs. The furniture looked expensive and luxurious; it felt like walking into a five-star hotel.

There was something that cut into the fantasy setting, though—and that would be the horde of police officers and the caution tape barring off the outdoor patio. There were also several employees being spoken to by officers, and one in particular—a young man in a fancy-looking waiter outfit—seemed particularly shaken up. He was trembling as a police officer offered him comfort.

Lily focused on getting to the crime scene. Flashing their badges, they were allowed entrance to the outdoor patio, and they stepped under the caution tape where a team of officers were still taking photos. They stepped back when Lily and Xander came in.

And there she was. The woman from the photo, lying there on a chair, staring out at the beach with dead eyes. There was no doubt she was deceased, and Lily's heart hurt for this girl. This was Veronica Smith, a girl who had a name, a life, a family… snuffed out by some killer. Lily's fists clenched.

She took a closer look at the body. There were no visible wounds… did she die of poisoning or something else? It was all very deliberate staging, like the man who'd put her here wanted her to appear alive. And it had worked for a while, apparently.

Moreover, there was a half-empty blue margarita on the table, but Lily was fairly certain the woman hadn't drunk it—unless it was what killed her?

Lily turned to a group of officers standing by. "Make sure forensics examines the contents of this drink," she said.

The officers nodded. It was a safety precaution; chances were, Veronica had died of asphyxiation too, like Grace had, but if that were the case, the killer had done it in such a way to not damage her face.

"Are you the FBI agents?" someone asked, and Lily and Xander turned to see a tall man wearing a police chief's badge.

Lily nodded. "I'm Agent Lily Dawn, this is my partner, Agent Xander Jackson."

"I'm Chief Graystone of the Ashlyn PD," he said, his face grim. The chief was a tall man with wisps of gray hair around his temples and lined wrinkles on his forehead. He wore a black shirt with the police department's insignia, and his brown eyes stared out with a determined look. He had a stern demeanor that brooked no nonsense and no doubt instilled respect in the officers around him. "I'm glad you two are here," he said, stepping up and looking at the body. "We… we don't see a lot of crime like this around here."

"I'd imagine you don't," Xander said, glancing at Veronica's body. "We're gonna need the low-down on what happened here."

"She was found here by a waiter, Mikael Nilsson—we kept him here, so you can go talk to him." The chief pointed inside at the young man Lily had noticed earlier. That made sense—he was the one who'd found the body.

"We'll go talk to him," Lily said. She turned back to the chief and gave him a nod. "Thank you for your help."

The chief nodded, then stepped aside as Lily and Xander walked back inside. As they passed through the lobby, they made their way over to Mikael Nilsson, the witness. He was sitting in a chair near the entrance, his eyes wide with fear and worry. He had a slight tremor in his hands as he nervously twisted them.

"Mr. Nilsson," Lily said softly, her voice gentle but authoritative. "I'm Agent Dawn, this is Agent Jackson of the FBI." She flashed her badge at him before slipping it back into her pocket.

Mikael's face softened slightly when he saw the FBI badges—he seemed relieved that someone was here who could help make sense of what had happened here today.

"O-of course," he stammered. "God, it's so awful… that poor girl!"

"Can you walk us through exactly what happened?" Lily asked.

"Well, I started my shift at noon, and it's not unusual for people to stick around for hours and get drunk, even early in the day, so when I came in and saw the woman sitting there with her half-empty drink, I figured she was still working on it, but… then as my shift went on, I noticed she hadn't moved, hadn't ordered anything. I got a bit worried. So I went and talked to her, but then…" He shuddered. "A bird flew in and stole her sunglasses right off her face, and that was when I realized she was, you know… dead."

"That must have been hard to witness," Lily said. "And the drink at her table—do you know who served it?"

"Everyone agrees it was left over from the table before," he said, then pointed at a girl who was standing with two other employees, looking shaken. "Talk to that redhead over there, that's Cherry. She made the drink."

"Thank you, Mikael. Please stay here in case we need to talk to you again."

Lily and Xander went over to the redhead, who looked up at them with confused green eyes. The other girls with her also looked nervous. Xander asked, "Afternoon, ladies. We hear you made the drink at the table?"

"I made it," Cherry said, and another girl—a blonde—chimed in.

"I served it to a table who left this morning," she said.

"It was the only blue margarita made today," said Cherry.

Lily nodded. "So it was just a leftover drink that hadn't been cleared, and the woman was staged with it?"

The girls nodded. "We think so."

"Are there any security cameras around here?" Xander asked.

The girls shook their heads. "No, it's like… a privacy thing," Cherry said. "We get some really rich customers here, and so we try very hard to respect their privacy."

"Not so good now that there's been a murder here," Xander said, and Lily shot him a look. This wasn't the time or place to be getting sarcastic.

"We'll have to look around the beach," Lily said, addressing the girls again. "Maybe there are clues outside. Do you know of any spots we should check out?"

The girls all shook their heads, but then one of them spoke up. "There's a spot where people go to watch the sun rise over the ocean," she said. "It's kind of hidden away at the end of the beach—it might be worth checking."

Lily and Xander thanked them for their help, then stepped outside into the bright sunshine. As they walked down to the beach, Lily glanced around for any signs that someone had been here recently—any footprints in the sand or discarded items—but it all looked relatively untouched. Still, they decided to take a closer look and set off toward the spot where they were told people usually watched sunrises.

The closer they got, the more apparent it became that this spot was well-loved by local beachgoers: two large wooden benches faced directly toward a stunning view of pink-orange sky as far as they could see out over the rolling waves. The horizon seemed almost too perfect to be real; it was like something out of a painting.

"What are we looking for, exactly?" Xander asked.

"I don't know," Lily said, "anything. The killer had the girl facing the beach—maybe there was a reason for that."

"I doubt it, but whatever," Xander said.

Maybe Lily's gut was off, but she felt like there could be a clue somewhere around here.

Just then, she noticed a blue lump in the sand near her feet. She bent down to take a closer look and saw that it was a thick winter scarf, likely made of cotton. She pulled it out of the sand.

"The hell is that thing?" Xander asked.

"It's… a scarf?" Lily asked.

That was odd. This was Florida, why would somebody have a scarf here? She dusted it off and rolled it up, then tucked it into her pocket.

"That's nasty," Xander said. "Why are you keeping that thing?"

"It could be significant," Lily said. "I don't know. Just a feeling."

"Whatever, weirdo."

She shot him a glare, then sighed. Maybe this was a clue, maybe it wasn't, but they'd better get back on track.

According to the file, Veronica's family was here at the resort. They were the ones Lily needed to talk to next.

CHAPTER FOUR

He hated them.

All of them.

As he sat in the bushes, his body weighed down by the many layers of clothing he wore, he watched the people on the beach roaming around half-naked like animals. Then there was him, overheating, always burning up… burning… he hated it.

He hated them.

He watched a shirtless man chase after a woman in a bikini. Sick. They all made him sick. Roaming around, showing so much skin… they were pathetic.

They didn't know what it was like to work to survive. No, they were all narcissists, feeding off attention, wearing next to no clothes just to gain a few looks from people who would never be relevant to them.

But one of them would die soon. The question was: which one?

Would it be the man who was hitting the volleyball over the net? Or the girl sprawled out shirtless under the sun, tanning her skin, ruining it? Why would anyone want to willingly burn themselves? That was what he didn't understand the most.

All these young people, these beautiful people; they didn't deserve what they had. They took advantage of it. They wasted it.

They didn't understand what he knew, what he had seen. They didn't realize that all it takes is one moment to change your life forever.

One moment. One mistake. One terrible decision.

They didn't know. They didn't know…

As he looked at them, he felt the anger burning through his skin. He wanted to take his knife out, the knife that he always carried, and cut them all open, spilling their guts all over the sand.

But he would not.

He would wait for the right time.

He would wait for the right moment.

One of them would die.

One of them deserved it.

He hated them.

They all deserved it.

All of these beautiful people with their pathetic little lives.

As he watched the beach, more people came and went, more bodies to choose from, more women in skimpy outfits, letting the sun's rays burn their precious skin. What he would give to have what they had.

He felt the rage burning more inside him, so much he had to turn away. No—he had to stay calm, as much as he wanted to watch the whole world burn. He had to wait for the right moment, and choose the right victim. They all deserved what was coming to them, but the most important thing was that he could not get caught.

His mind and body were already prisons.

He couldn't get put in a real one.

But he had to do this. He had to make them pay, to show the world that their obsession with "beauty" was pointless and futile. Beauty would not save them.

Not from him.

He focused again and gazed at the crowd, looking for the one he was going to take.

He didn't know how he was going to do it—maybe he would slip a drug into their drink, or maybe he would just cut them up with his knife. It didn't matter. He just knew he had to take one of them.

And he wanted to make sure they suffered.

Because they didn't know what they had. They didn't know.

He watched them all, a sea of beautiful people, and he hated them.

He hated them all.

Then, as he focused on the crowd, he saw her.

She was beautiful.

She looked like them—young, hot, wearing a bikini—but she didn't fit in like the others.

She was crying.

He watched her, standing on the beach, sobbing in the sand, wiping her tears with the back of her hand, before she threw her face into her other hand, sobbing even more.

What a pathetic, vile girl. He could only assume she was crying because one of the stupid boys she required validation from had rejected her. What a hard life, being so beautiful. He almost laughed.

He saw her watching one of the boys—a tall, muscled young man—as he was talking to other women.

Maybe this would be his next lucky pick.

But then he saw another man… shirtless, his ab muscles even more prominent than the other man's. He walked up to the crying girl and offered her a hug, which she accepted.

As he observed them, he built a story in his head. This man was trying to be this girl's prince charming… to be a nice guy… but no, what he really was was a predator, picking up the pieces left behind by the other man, using this girl's pathetic sadness for his own gains.

As he watched them, he began to hate them both, and in that moment, he made up his mind.

He had chosen his target.

CHAPTER FIVE

Lily took a breath as she knocked on the door that the Smiths were staying in. She stole a quick look at Xander, who also had a tight expression; talking to the parents of murder victims was never a fun time.

Moments later, a middle-aged woman with dark hair like Veronica opened the door. She had makeup streaming down her face and was wearing a sundress, but the air of wealth was instant. Behind her stood a man in his sixties with white hair and suntanned skin.

"Mr. and Mrs. Smith?" Lily asked. "I'm Agent Dawn with the FBI, and this is my partner, Agent Jackson. May we come in?"

"Tell me you found who did it," Mrs. Smith said. "Tell me—you found who killed my daughter, right?"

Lily's stomach twisted. This was going to be a doozy, wasn't it? "No, ma'am, not yet. May we please come in?"

Mrs. Smith stepped back and gestured to the two agents, her face still a mask of grief. Xander and Lily entered the room and were immediately struck by its opulence. Everything was gold, from the gilded furniture to the shimmering curtains that hung from floor-to-ceiling windows. A crystal chandelier sparkled above them, refracting light in every direction and illuminating the plush rugs that lined the floor.

The Smiths had clearly spared no expense when it came to their accommodations; everything was pristinely kept and smelled faintly of lavender and roses. Two couches were arranged around a coffee table in one corner, with several stacks of magazines neatly arranged on top. Across from them was an enormous flat-screen television mounted on the wall with a sleek sound system beneath it.

"Please," Mrs. Smith said, her voice wavering slightly as she motioned for them to sit down on one of the couches. "Make yourselves comfortable." She sat down across from them in an armchair, her husband standing beside her with his hand resting gently on her shoulder.

Lily nodded gratefully as she settled into one of the cushions, Xander beside her.

"First of all, I'm sorry for your loss," Lily said.

"She was our little girl," Mr. Smith managed, and he turned away, choking up. Mrs. Smith hugged him, sobbing more.

"We want to find out who did this," Lily assured them. "We're going to. But we need to know everything about your daughter, where she was last seen—everything."

"We saw her last night!" Mrs. Smith exclaimed. "She went to bed in her room, then in the morning, she was gone! I thought she went down to the beach or something, but then hours later, a police officer came here and said—"

She stopped herself. Lily could tell this was awful for her.

She wanted her daughter's killer to pay, but she also wanted that justice to come swiftly and without pain. She was sitting on the edge of her seat, her hands clenched together in her lap, sobbing silently.

Mr. Smith still had his arm around his wife's shoulder. The two were clearly in love, but the sheer magnitude of their grief was overwhelming.

"We're going to find who did this," she said. "I'm sure of it. But we need your help. If you could tell me about Veronica and her friends—where she hangs out, where she was last seen, who she was with, if she had any enemies, anything like that—it would be very helpful. Everything you can think of."

The Smiths looked at each other and then back at the agents. "Veronica didn't have any enemies," Mrs. Smith said. "She was a good girl. She always listened, she always did what we said, she never did anything to hurt anyone. She was just a good girl."

"Was she spending a lot of time with anyone here at the resort?" Xander asked. "Any boys who maybe took a liking to her?"

"Not at all," Mrs. Smith said. "We came down here from New York to get away for a while. Veronica was here to spend time with us and made it clear she didn't want to meet any boys. She has a lot of them roaming around her back home, and this was her break from that."

Suddenly, Mr. Smith stood up, desperation in his eyes. "Please, you can find who did this, right? You won't give up? We can pay you—we can—"

"You don't need to pay us, sir," Lily said, "this is our job."

"You can pay us by helping us understand everything we need to know about your kid," Xander cut in. "Please sit back down, sir."

Deflating, Mr. Smith sat down next to his wife.

"So we have the story straight," Lily said, "you don't know where Veronica went or when she left her room?"

"Yes, we just know she was gone before we were awake at nine a.m., so it was before that," Mrs. Smith explained. "As for who our daughter was, well…" She took out a phone and opened it up, then came over to Lily and showed her the screen.

On it was a social media profile—a series of photos of Veronica, looking like a fashion model. Most of the photos showed Veronica with very little clothing, exposing a lot of skin.

"She was so beautiful," Mr. Smith said. "She was so beautiful…"

Lily swallowed, watching the old man's eyes well up. He didn't even look like he was talking about his daughter; he looked like he was talking about his wife who had passed away.

"She was a model," Mrs. Smith said, "but not in the same way other models are. She modeled for a few companies, but she also had a blog where she posted a lot of her outfits and her travels. Her followers were very proud of her."

"And she was beautiful," Mr. Smith agreed. "Always so beautiful, that was our V."

"But…she wasn't that kind of model," Mrs. Smith said. "She wasn't doing these photos for money. She wasn't doing this for money. She did it for fun. She did it for herself. We were supposed to spend a few days here, just relax and enjoy each other's company at this beautiful resort," she went on, "and she was going to take pictures of her vacation, and some of her modeling outfits, that kind of thing. It's what she did."

"Her modeling is what she did to relax," Mr. Smith said. "She was so beautiful, and she loved the attention. She loved the camera."

"She loved being in the public eye," Mrs. Smith agreed. "She loved making people smile."

"She was very popular," Mr. Smith said. "She had a lot of followers on her blog, and on her social media, though she didn't really interact with people personally."

Lily thought back to Grace Maloney, the first victim, who was found at a different resort about an hour away from here. Grace was a social media influencer by trade, but Veronica only used it for fun.

Still, they both had followings, and they could be significant. It was definitely a connection Lily wanted to know more about.

They had likely gathered all they could from the Smiths for now, so Lily stood up. "Thank you both for your time. Please don't leave the resort until we have this sorted out. We'll be in touch."

"Please, you have to find who did this," Mr. Smith said, pleading. "She was our only daughter. We can't rest until we know what happened to her."

Lily nodded solemnly. "I promise you, I will find who killed your daughter. You have my word."

She gave the Smiths one last glance before turning to leave with Xander. As they walked away, Lily silently vowed that she would do everything in her power to bring justice for Veronica and her family. She knew it wouldn't be easy, but she was determined to make sure that whoever did this would pay for what they had done.

Lily and Xander continued down the hallway of the resort, and Xander said, "So, what do we think about all this so far? Any guesses on who the killer might be?"

"Well, both are beautiful women who were into social media," Lily said. "Maybe an obsessed fan?"

"Could be that kind of weirdo, yeah."

It all didn't seem right to Lily, though. Why go through the trouble of staging the women like they were still alive? And how exactly did he choose them?

Lily took a moment to build up a profile. They were looking for a man, most likely… maybe a man who hated women.

He wanted to show that women were not in control, and he wanted to prove it by taking away their lives. He was a bit of a loner, someone who wouldn't draw attention to himself. He was patient enough to wait for his victims to be alone.

But most importantly, he was smart. He knew how to play with people's emotions, how to make them think they were safe when they weren't. They were looking for a master manipulator who could hide behind false personas and get away with murder without anyone suspecting him until it was too late.

He had some kind of fascination with them, and a desire to control them. He killed them in such a way that they almost seemed alive. That could be why he was so meticulous about their appearances.

He was most likely someone who had the ability to travel between the resorts unnoticed, which meant he was probably well-off or connected in some way. Lily knew she needed more evidence before jumping to conclusions, but she couldn't help but feel like all these clues were leading somewhere.

Whoever this killer was, Lily was determined to find him and bring him to justice. This was why she lived, why she worked so hard—to stop people like this.

Whoever he was, wherever he was, he would not get away with it.

CHAPTER SIX

"Agents, I'm glad you're here," Chief Graystone said, welcoming Lily and Xander into the Ashlyn police department. It was small, but swanky for a police station, which Lily would expect for a community with so many mansions in it. It was surprisingly well-kept with modern, glossy furniture and spotless floors. The walls were decorated with professional-looking portraits of police officers in their uniforms and a few awards given by the community. The officers on duty looked sharp in their uniforms. It was obvious that this station catered to a wealthy community with its high-end amenities.

But all Lily wanted was to get to a private spot to get some research done.

"Thank you for having us, Chief," Lily said as he guided them up the hall. "We're gonna need to access every file on both victims—Grace and Veronica."

"We have a briefing room you two can take over for as long as you need," the chief said, leading them farther up the narrow corridor.

Xander let out a whistle. "Pretty fancy cop shop y'all have around here."

The chief chuckled. "You get used to it."

Finally, they reached a large door at the end of the hallway. The chief pushed it open to reveal a spacious and modernly decorated conference room with a long table in the middle surrounded by sleek office chairs.

"This is where we brief our officers and go over any evidence that we find," the chief said, gesturing for them to sit. "It should give you two plenty of privacy while you work."

"This is perfect," Lily said as she walked inside, looking around in awe. It was just what she needed to get her work done without any distractions.

"I'll let you two get to work," Chief Graystone said before turning around and heading back down the hall.

Lily and Xander took their seats at either side of the table and opened their laptops, ready to begin their investigation into who had committed such an atrocious crime against two innocent women.

"First things first, we should look more into Grace Maloney," Lily said. "We know she was twenty-nine, a social media influencer, self-made by selling products to her followers…"

"But we need to know more about who she actually was," Xander said in agreement.

Lily pulled up her search engine and typed in Grace's name. A lot of information came up, including her social media accounts, public appearances, interviews, and more. Lily read through each article she found with rapt attention, trying to get a better understanding of the woman behind the influencer persona.

She discovered that Grace had grown up in a small town in Wyoming before moving to Asheville, North Carolina, when she was eighteen to pursue her dreams of becoming an entrepreneur. She had been successful ever since, having built a following from scratch by providing helpful advice and products that solved people's everyday problems. She had come to Florida on vacation, but still lived in North Carolina.

Lily stopped on a photo of Grace—staring back at Lily from beyond death's veil—but it was also strangely beautiful in its own way, almost as if she were still alive somewhere out there just waiting for justice to be served. Lily swore to herself that she'd stop the man who did this.

Switching gears, Lily turned away from who Grace was and focused on where she was killed. Little Tropic was a resort farther north up the beach, about an hour away, so it was reasonable to think the killer could have just driven or taken a boat.

"We need to look into people who were staying at both resorts," Lily said. "Someone who was there at the time both girls were killed."

"Info's not in the database yet," Xander said. "I was just looking into that."

"What?" Lily frowned. She pulled up the database, and sure enough, there weren't customer logs for the last twenty-four hours.

"That place is huge," Xander said. "It's a lot of names."

"And we need them now."

Lily wasn't sure what to do… she didn't want to wait around for all the names to come through—she needed that information expedited!

Her mind raced over the possibilities. If they knew who was staying at each resort at the right time of the murders, then that would narrow down the list.

On a whim, she thought of something.

"Can we ask Chief Aboye to get it expedited?"

"What?" Xander asked. "I mean, maybe, but I don't like to pester the chief when I'm on a case."

"It's worth a shot." Lily took out her phone and called Chief Aboye.

Lily bit her lip as she dialed the chief's number, hoping she'd be willing to help.

"Agent Dawn?" Chief Aboye's smooth voice came in on the other line.

"Chief," Lily said, "I'm sorry to bother you, but I need some help. We're trying to narrow down a list of people who were at each resort at the times of the killings, but it's a lot of names, and they haven't updated the database yet."

"Hmm, it should be all in there," the chief said. "Let me make some calls, see if I can get that information put in stat."

"Thank you," Lily said, her heart beating fast.

She felt like she was running out of time before the next victim would be claimed.

Lily put her phone away and let out a sigh of relief. "That was a close one."

"But we still don't know if it'll help," Xander said.

"It's better than nothing."

Until they had those lists, they were stuck.

Lily took the time waiting to look into Grace again. She pulled up the photos of Grace's crime scene; like Veronica, she'd been staged like she was alive, on a chair, with a hat on. Lily thought about what kind of statement this made. Was the killer asserting dominance over the women, showing he could do anything with them? What motivation would he have to leave them like this? It had to mean something.

Lily dug deeper, looking for any other connections between the victims to see if there was anything they had in common that could point to a motive. Both were young, attractive women in their twenties; both were found at resorts far away from home. But then Lily noticed something else: both Grace and Veronica were wearing dresses that were similar in style and color. When looking at photos of them side by side, it seemed like they were almost identical.

It was strange, but it made Lily think even harder about what the killer's motivations could be. Was he trying to make some kind of statement with his victims? Was he sending a message that these women weren't as important as they thought? Or maybe this was all some sort of twisted game to him—a way for him to assert power over the women by controlling their clothing choices.

Whatever his reasons, Lily knew one thing for certain: she was going to find out who this killer was and why he did it. She would not rest until justice had been served for Grace and Veronica. And hopefully, no one else would have to die before they caught him.

When Lily's phone rang, she snatched it up. "It's the chief," she told Xander, and he looked up hopefully from his screen.

"Chief?" Lily asked.

"Agent Dawn, the information you need should be in the database now," the chief said. "Cross-reference those names. I expect results soon."

Lily nodded, feeling emboldened. "You can count on us, Chief."

They hung up, and Lily shot Xander a smile. "We've got our list."

***

After going through the names and cross-referencing them all, Lily and Xander found a match.

Still in the briefing room at the Ashlyn PD, Lily and Xander leaned eagerly in front of Lily's laptop, reading the information over and over. Lily couldn't believe it—this might really turn out to be their guy.

Roger Pearson.

He was at the other resort at the time Grace was killed.

On top of that, he was at the Ashlyn resort yesterday—he had checked out in the morning, before Veronica's body was discovered, and even stranger—the record showed that he had driven from Ashlyn right back to Little Tropic and had checked in only a few hours ago.

The timeline was perfect.

"Shit, this could really be him," Xander said.

"Agreed," Lily said, but she swiped her fingers over the keyboard. "First, though, we need to see if this guy has a criminal record."

Lily's search revealed that Roger Pearson had an extensive criminal record. He had been convicted of multiple counts of petty theft and burglary, and had even served time for a violent assault. His most recent arrest was for breaking and entering, but the charges were dropped due to lack of evidence.

But this wasn't all—Lily also discovered that according to the police reports, Roger Pearson often worked in tandem with a group of criminals known as the "Tropic Thieves," who specialized in targeting tourists at resorts along the coast.

It seemed that Lily and Xander had finally found their man—now they just needed to find out how he was connected to Grace's and Veronica's murders before anyone else got hurt.

CHAPTER SEVEN

In the passenger seat of the rental car, Lily sat back while Xander had the wheel, mulling over the details of the case. They sped down the Florida highway as the late afternoon sun created a painting on the horizon. The highway stretched ahead like an undulating ribbon, glittering in the golden hues of the setting sun. The sky was a canvas of orange and pink, fading into an inky blue. The clouds resembled brushstrokes, blending together as they evaporated into the dusk. A faint fragrance of salt and sand wafted through the air as they drove through the balmy sea breeze.

These girls, Grace and Veronica… they had been on vacation, in paradise, when the killer had taken them. How was he doing it? How could he have taken them right under everyone's nose? Maybe there was just so much going on, so many people, that no one noticed. People tend to not be on guard while in paradise; it's a fantasy place, an alternate reality where you can bury your fears and forget the world outside of the beautiful resort.

And yet a killer had slipped into two of them now. Lily could only assume he wouldn't stop.

She stole a glance at Xander as he drove. He'd been quiet, quiet for him, anyway, and Lily wondered what he thought about all of this, or what he had going on in his life outside of work. She remembered the phone call he'd had on their last case; a call he never elaborated on, but had seemed concerned about. It was really none of Lily's business; she didn't like when he pried into her, so she wouldn't pry into him. Still, it piqued her curiosity.

They drove in silence for a long time, and as Lily gazed out at the sands, she thought of her parents back home in Aruba. She'd left her belongings to show them that she had every intention of returning, but she could tell by their reaction that they were disappointed she'd returned home, only to leave immediately.

But it couldn't be helped. Lily was an FBI agent. This was what she did.

As they were driving, Lily's phone rang. Xander glanced at her before focusing on the road. Curious, Lily took it out, expecting some sort of news—but a number she hadn't seen in a long time flashed on her screen.

Frank Foster.

As in, Special Agent Frank Foster, Lily's original partner with the FBI—the man who had retired a couple of years ago. Since then, Lily had cycled through three different partners plus Xander, but no one had ever stuck the way Foster had.

In truth, he'd been her mentor. A gruff, older man who always smelled like whiskey and smoke, but he was a hell of an agent with a long career. He'd been in homicide in New York in his thirties before he switched to the FBI, and he'd brought a unique set of skills, considering where he'd spent much of his life. Of course, that was before Lily was even born.

By the time she'd ended up with Foster, he was at the end of his career. The last case they ever worked on together was taking down the deadliest killer Lily had seen to this day.

Vincent Gould.

It was a grueling case, terrifying and frustrating, as the killer's movements seemed to elude even the most experienced agents and detectives before Lily and Foster were put on the case. He'd been killing women and keeping their toes as trophies, but doing it in such a sporadic way that it was impossible to track who he would choose; children, elderly, no one was safe. But Foster had pushed them on, giving Lily the confidence that they could do this job, that they could take down the killer—and eventually they did.

It had been some of the most intense hours of Lily's life, and she remembered every detail like it was yesterday. She thought back to hunting down leads, questioning suspects, and collecting evidence until finally bringing in enough to issue an arrest warrant.

Foster had stayed with her through it all. He'd been there when they issued the warrant and pulled Vincent out of his home in handcuffs. He'd been there when he confessed everything under pressure from their team. And he'd been there when everything was over—finally putting an end to one of Virginia's worst serial killers ever.

Lily remembered it all so vividly: the nightmarish moments chasing after him, the fear that coursed through her veins when she thought he was going to get away, the overwhelming sense of relief when they finally arrested him. And most importantly, she would never forget how proud Foster had been when they handed over their file to the authorities and put an end to this madman's reign of terror.

Vincent was still locked away in prison and would remain there for the rest of his life.

After that, Foster retired. Lily had been beyond disappointed. He was her mentor, and she'd doubted if she could do this without him. But she'd pushed on, making a name for herself independently of Foster. But she never forgot his teachings.

Why on earth was he calling her now?

"You gonna answer that?" Xander asked, prompting Lily to snap out of it. She looked down at the name and swallowed the lump in her throat, then answered the phone.

"This is Agent Dawn."

"Dawn. It's Foster."

Hearing his gruff voice gave her so many memories. She pictured him sitting in a chair with a glass of scotch. "Special Agent Foster," she managed, gaining a look from Xander. "What's going on?"

"Sorry to throw this at you, kiddo." He sighed through the phone. "I'm trying to enjoy my retirement, but you know, once you join the FBI, you never really leave. Not till you're dead."

The thought made Lily's stomach roil.

"Foster, what's going on?"

"It's Gould."

Lily's heart nearly stopped. "What about him?"

"He's making threats against us from prison, saying he's gonna bust you and make us pay—I got a call from a guard there, an old buddy of mine, who says the guy's still holding a grudge hard against us, and he's galvanizing other inmates with tales about how we need to pay."

"What the hell?" Lily said. "He's locked up. What can he do to us?"

"Nothing," Foster said. "Well, hopefully nothing. I'm a bit concerned about how much information about us he's been allegedly giving other inmates, some who might get out long before he does."

Lily's nerves pinched. This was also part of the job—making enemies.

"He can't hurt us," Lily said. "He'll never get out of jail."

She felt Xander glance at her again. She felt exposed having to have this conversation with Xander right beside her. She might be more vulnerable if she was in private to talk to Foster, but with Xander here…

"I just want to make sure you're safe, kiddo." She could hear the concern in his voice, and she was grateful he was looking out for her. Because Lily didn't want to think about Vincent Gould getting out of prison and looking for revenge.

"I'm always safe," Lily said. "Don't worry about me. I'm more worried about you. But he won't get out of prison. It's maximum security, so I have no idea how he'd pull that off."

"I don't know," Foster said. "He's pretty smart. Always has been."

Lily felt a huge weight on her shoulders. She'd helped put Vincent Gould behind bars. Now he was threatening her.

"I'll keep my eyes open," Foster said. "I'm sure he won't do anything, but I don't want to take any chances. I'm gonna be around for a little while longer, but if anything happens…"

Lily shuddered. "I know. It's okay."

"I'm just worried about you, kid."

"I know," Lily assured him. "You don't have to worry about me. I'm always careful."

"I know you are," Foster said. "But I just want to make sure you're okay."

Lily sighed. She knew what he was thinking. She also knew that she didn't want to have this conversation with him over the phone. She'd rather it be face to face. But at the same time, maybe it was best that she didn't, because it was hard to be all professional when she was talking to Foster, and she was more concerned about being all business.

"I'll be fine," she said. "You don't need to worry about me. Thanks for the call."

"You got it. Stay safe out there, kid."

With that, the call ended. Lily's heart pulled as she stared down at her phone.

"What was that about?" Xander asked.

She glanced at him. For a moment, she'd almost forgotten he was there. Maybe she owed him an explanation—they were partners, after all, but this situation was… complicated, and she'd rather not go into great detail.

"It's a guy my old partner and I put away," Lily said. "He's making threats against us from prison. My old partner just wanted me to know."

"Ah, shit," Xander said. "What kind of threats?"

Lily looked away. "He's gonna bust us and make us pay."

"Shit," Xander said.

Lily looked back at him. "I know. It's just… my old partner was kind of worried. This Vincent guy is pretty dangerous. He might know stuff about us."

Xander sighed. "That's not good."

"No," Lily said. "It's not."

"You don't sound too worried, though."

She shrugged. "This is my job. I'm used to it."

"Doesn't make it any less scary when you've got some crazy son of a bitch who wants you dead. Trust me, I've got my share under my belt too."

Lily thought back to how much she'd worried about this when she was assigned to work with Foster. He'd made it clear that she was valuable to him, and that she could rely on him to protect her when needed.

Now, though, she was on her own. Foster was retired. Of course there was Xander, but their partnership was still so new.

And even though the thought made her a little nervous, she trusted herself to take care of herself. She had the skills and the knowledge—and Xander didn't have to know about Vincent Gould.

"I'll be all right," she assured him.

"I know you will," Xander said. "And I'm here if you need me."

Lily nodded. "Thanks, partner."

"No problem," Xander said.

They looked at each other for a moment. Lily felt a flutter in her chest. *Weird,* she thought, passing it off.

Focusing on the road ahead, Lily saw they were getting close. She tucked her thoughts of Foster and Vincent Gould away—it was time to focus on the case.

The killer just might be in that resort.

CHAPTER EIGHT

The Little Tropic resort was more modest than Ashlyn's—but Lily was still amazed by how extravagant it was. The resort was nestled at the bottom of lush, tropical hills, its bright white buildings with red-tiled roofs glimmering in the sun. The grounds were meticulously manicured, with multiple gardens and fountains dotting the landscape. Brightly colored flowers bloomed in every direction and palm trees swayed in the balmy breeze. Everywhere Lily looked there were hammocks, pools, and chairs where people were lounging and enjoying themselves.

Sweet floral notes combined with salty ocean spray filled Lily's nose as she breathed in deeply. The air was heavy with humidity, but there was something else too—a unique blend of spices that reminded her of home.

Lily and Xander entered the resort's main lobby. Unlike Ashlyn, this crime scene had already been handled and the resort was trying its best to get back into the swing of things, but Lily had a feeling there were fewer people around than usual.

They walked up to the main desk, where a woman sat at a computer. She looked up with a friendly smile.

"Hi there, welcome to Little Tropic resort! How can I help you?"

Lily held up her badge, along with Xander. "I'm Agent Lily Dawn with the FBI, and this is my partner, Agent Xander Jackson."

"Oh my," the girl said. "This is about what happened, isn't it?"

"Talking about the murder?" Xander asked.

Grimly, the girl nodded. "We've been trying to recover, but… it was quite traumatic for everyone, guests and staff. Myself included."

"I imagine it would be," Lily said. "We're actually here looking for a specific guest. His name is Roger Pearson. He should've checked in earlier today."

The girl frowned. "Let me just check the system…" She tapped on her keyboard for a few moments before looking up. "Yes, here he is. Room 207."

"Thank you," Lily said, giving her an appreciative smile.

The girl gave them a polite nod in return. "Good luck with whatever it is you're looking for, and let me know if there's anything else I can help with."

Lily and Xander thanked her, then turned to leave. They made their way up the grand staircase to the second floor, where they came upon a hallway filled with doors. Lily counted off until she found 207.

She knocked on the door softly, but there was no answer. She glanced at Xander, who shrugged his shoulders in response.

"Maybe he's not here," Lily said, turning to look around the hall for any signs of life. But it was eerily quiet—not a single guest or staff member in sight.

Lily looked back at the door and decided to give it one more try just in case Roger was in there but wasn't answering. She knocked louder this time, but still nothing happened. With a sigh, she stepped back from the door and let out a breath she hadn't realized she'd been holding. She couldn't give up, not yet, not when she was so close.

She knocked harder—and as she did so, the door gently pushed open. Lily exchanged a confused look with Xander. It looked like he hadn't locked his door, and they couldn't pass the opportunity to check inside. The room was empty and there was no sign of Roger Pearson anywhere save for the zipped suitcase on the floor. The bed was neatly made, with no signs of a struggle or anything else out of place.

"Looks like he's not here," Lily said to Xander with some disappointment in her voice. "Let's keep looking elsewhere."

Xander nodded in agreement and they started making their way back down the hall toward the lobby once more—hoping to find Roger Pearson and get some answers.

Lily checked her phone and pulled up the photo they had of Roger—his mugshot showing an overweight, balding white man with sunken-in eyes. He was a thief by trade, of course, and Lily could infer that was where he'd gotten the money to be staying at these resorts. This was who they were looking for.

"He could be anywhere," Lily said. "Let's check by the pool."

They followed the signs to the pool area, a large open space with beautifully landscaped gardens, lounge chairs and umbrellas scattered around it. A few people were lounging in the sun, but there was no sign of Roger Pearson. Lily scanned the area carefully, but she knew he wasn't there.

She sighed and looked at Xander. "Let's keep looking."

Lily and Xander kept searching—scanning the faces of all the guests gathered near the pool, looking for any sign of recognition or familiarity in Roger's features. But it seemed as though their search was fruitless; there was no trace of him anywhere.

"Where the hell could he be?" Xander said.

Lily frowned as they began walking back toward the lobby. "I don't know. But we can't give up so easily. This is a serious case. We've got to keep looking."

Xander sighed. "I know, I know. But where do we look? This resort must have hundreds of guests and staff, and the man we're looking for is the only one we can identify. It's not like he left us a trail to follow."

Lily stopped. She looked around her, taking in the resort's surroundings once more. There was a tall hedge nearby, lush and verdant. The resort had a garden full of bright, colorful flowers, and a few of the bushes around the hedge were blooming. The sweet scent of flowers was in the air, and Lily breathed in the fragrance deeply.

It was getting late, around dinner time, and they couldn't afford to spend any more time dillydallying. A thought occurred to her—the other resort did not have any cameras, but this one just might. "Let's see if they have any security cameras at all," Lily said.

Xander nodded in agreement and they went to the front desk to ask. The same girl as before looked up at them with hope.

"Did you find what you were looking for?" she asked.

"No, actually," Lily said. "We can't locate Roger anywhere. Do you have security footage?"

The girl nodded and motioned for them to follow her. They trailed her down the hallway until they reached a small room filled with screens and computers.

"This is our security center," she said, pointing to the various monitors displaying different parts of the resort. "You can use this to check if someone's been here recently, but I'm afraid the cameras are only on the public areas."

Lily looked at all the screens and pointed to one in particular. "Can we see that one?" she asked, pointing to a monitor showing the entrance of the resort.

The girl nodded and typed something into the computer. The footage flashed back to earlier that day, and sure enough, there was Roger Pearson walking through the main doors of the resort. He was carrying a bag with him and wearing an old pair of jeans and an untucked shirt. “That’s him,” Lily said with a satisfied nod as she watched Roger enter the lobby area. ”So he was here. Did he leave?”

They checked the later footage too, but Roger was never seen leaving the resort—which had to mean he was still here somewhere.

“Let’s check the other areas,” Lily said, pointing to another monitor. This one showed the entrance of a bathhouse, and sure enough, there was Roger walking in with his bag. The timestamp on the footage suggested it had been earlier that same day—less than an hour before they’d arrived at the resort.

“He must still be here,” Xander said, looking at Lily with determination. “Let’s go check it out.”

Lily and Xander made their way to the bathhouse, following the winding paths of the resort until they eventually arrived at its entrance. It was a large, two-story building with a wide balcony overlooking the pool area. They could see people lounging in the sun and swimming in the pool from up here, but there was no sign of Roger Pearson.

They entered the building and were immediately hit with a wave of warmth and humidity. The air was thick with steam and smelled of jasmine, eucalyptus, and lavender. A few people were scattered around the room, some lounging on cushioned benches while others soaked in one of the many hot tubs located throughout the space.

Lily and Xander continued to search for Roger as they made their way through each room of the bathhouse. There was a lot of space; he had to be around here somewhere.

“Let’s check the saunas,” Lily told Xander. Her hair was beginning to frizz up from being in there.

They went to the last room of the bathhouse, a long, narrow hallway filled with several saunas. Lily and Xander opened each one until they finally found what they were looking for: Roger Pearson lying motionless on one of the benches with a towel wrapped around his waist. What the…?

Lily’s stomach filled with dread as she and Xander stepped into the room.

He was pale, and his eyes were closed. He wasn’t moving. Lily’s heart froze in her chest as she slowly reached out to touch his arm—he was cold. In that moment, she knew he was gone.

Dead.

Their suspect was already dead.

CHAPTER NINE

Lily and Xander stood there in shock, unable to move or speak. This wasn't what Lily had expected to find. They had come here looking for answers, but instead they were met with a cold reality they hadn't anticipated.

Lily gingerly moved closer to the body and began to examine it, looking for any signs of foul play. She carefully inspected his face, arms, and legs for any bruises or cuts that could indicate he had been in a fight. His hands were cold and clammy, but there were no signs of struggle or injury.

She then looked at the towel wrapped around his waist for any tears or rips that might suggest he had been attacked. Again, there was nothing out of the ordinary.

Finally, Lily looked around the room for anything out of place—maybe a clue as to what had happened to Roger Pearson. But again she found nothing.

It seemed like there was no sign of foul play here—other than the fact that Roger Pearson was now dead in this sauna room. If she had to guess, it looked natural. Maybe the heat had gotten to him, even though he wasn't that old.

But Lily knew they couldn't be certain without a proper investigation. She looked at Xander with a heavy heart.

"We need to get the police in here," she said solemnly. "This is a crime scene now."

"Son of a bitch," Xander said. "Think he offed himself to avoid getting caught?"

"I don't know," Lily said. "It seems natural."

That was Lily's guess, anyway. It looked like he'd just passed out and died, maybe from the heat, maybe a heart attack. Lily had felt so sure that Roger was their guy, but seeing him like this… it made her feel for the man, no matter his history.

He was still a person, and his life was now over. That was never a pretty thing. Lily had seen a lot of death.

She had witnessed the deaths of criminals and innocents alike, some in her home country and some from other places she had visited. Some were peaceful, while others were violent. Some died surrounded by loved ones, while others died alone with no one to mourn them.

No matter the circumstances, all of these deaths impacted her. She had seen too much death in her life, and it took its toll on her spirit. It was moments like this that made her feel a deep sorrow for all those who had been taken away too soon.

From her years as an FBI agent, Lily had seen all kinds of death. Murders, suicides, accidents—she had seen them all. Every one of them was heartbreaking in its own way, and every one brought with it a reminder of the fragility of life.

She had been to countless crime scenes over the years, and each time she saw a body lying lifeless on the floor it filled her with sadness. Even when she knew that the person deserved what happened to them—whether through their own actions or someone else's—it still weighed heavily on her heart.

But there weren't any signs of violence or struggle here. It seemed like Roger Pearson had just passed away peacefully in his sleep. It made Lily feel differently about him; no matter what kind of man he was, his death deserved respect and recognition.

"Damn," Xander said. "Okay, gimme a sec, I'll call the cops and get them in here."

As Xander stepped away, Lily stared back at the body. This wasn't the way she'd expected this case to go, not at all—she'd expected to drag Roger in for questioning, maybe even arrest him for the murders…

But he was dead now. If he was the killer, then that was a good thing. But what if he wasn't?

This was a dead end, a dead body on a bench at a crime scene… and they weren't any closer to identifying the real killer.

Lily sighed and shook her head. What-ifs and maybes didn't matter now. What mattered was that she got the cops here to conduct an investigation. She moved away from the body and stood near the door, waiting for the police to arrive.

Lily rubbed her forehead. This was a nightmare.

Xander appeared in the door to the sauna. "They're on their way. Might as well get out of there, Dawn—no need for you to die from heat exhaustion too."

Lily nodded and stepped out of the hot, humid sauna into the slightly less humid main area of the bathhouse. Lily didn't know what to make of all this—all she knew was that if Roger was their killer, then that would be a good, if underwhelming, ending for it.

"We better go search his room again after the cops get here," Lily told Xander. "Maybe there's something we missed."

Xander nodded. "Better safe than sorry."

***

Lily unzipped the suitcase in Roger's hotel room and flipped it open, only to find nothing but poorly organized clothes—and a plastic bag full of money. The police had taken over the scene with Roger, and the bathhouse had been evacuated. So far, there was nothing to suggest Roger had been murdered, but the police would be covering all angles and report back as soon as they had information.

Until then, Lily needed to prove if Roger was—or wasn't—their killer.

Xander was scouring the closet when Lily looked over her shoulder and said, "Hey, check this out."

Xander came over and looked over her shoulder. He whistled. "That's a lot of dough. Can assume it was stolen."

"But none of this tells us he was our killer," Lily said.

"Nah. Let's keep looking."

The two of them continued to search the room, looking under the bed, in drawers, and behind paintings. They looked through the bathroom for any clues that could help them identify the killer. But no matter how hard they looked, there was nothing to be found.

After an hour of searching, Lily and Xander had still found nothing. No evidence that Roger Pearson was their man—or that he had anything to do with this case at all.

Lily sat down on the edge of the bed and sighed heavily. She felt like they were going around in circles. Nothing was adding up and she didn't know what else to do or where else to look for clues.

Xander stood by the window and looked out at the city below them. "Maybe we're missing something," he said finally. Lily shook her head slowly and closed her eyes as if praying for a miracle.

But even then, she knew it wouldn't come. Not for her.

This case was a wild goose chase, and it was making her head spin. Every step forward seemed to lead them two steps back, and Lily felt more and more distressed with every minute that passed. She was completely and utterly out of her depth. What if there was another killer still out there? If so, Roger was their best lead, and if he wasn't their man, then Lily had no idea where to go from there.

Xander put a hand on her shoulder. "Keep your chin up, Lily," he said reassuringly. "We'll figure this out."

Lily nodded, though she couldn't shake the feeling that they were missing something. Something important. But what?

"Something tells me Roger isn't the killer," Lily said. "I think he's still out there."

Xander turned to her and said, "Maybe we should retrace our steps. Go back over the case one more time."

Lily nodded. It was worth a try. At least then they would know if they had missed anything that could help them figure out who the real killer was. She rose from the bed and started walking toward the door, Xander following close behind her.

"Let's get to work," she said determinedly. She couldn't let her resolve falter.

Lily had worked a lot of cases in her time as an FBI agent. Even though she was only twenty-eight, she knew she was experienced, and while getting down sometimes was natural, she had to keep her spirit alive.

She had started her career as a rookie, but she had grown to become an expert in the field. She had worked on some of the most notorious cases and brought justice to many criminals. Even though it was hard work, she found solace in her accomplishments.

Lily had seen her fair share of heartbreak, too. The victims were always the hardest part of any case, and it took its toll emotionally. But while it was hard to witness such tragedy firsthand, Lily knew that with every criminal they put away, there was one less person out there wreaking havoc on innocent people's lives.

And that made all the hardships worth it in the end.

She was determined to break this case, and she knew that determination was the key to any success. She had been in harder spots before with more difficult cases, and while this one seemed to be getting the better of her, she knew that at the end of it all she could make it out alive.

Just as they were leaving the hotel room, Lily's phone buzzed, and she took it out.

It was Chief Aboye.

Her stomach dropped, and she shot Xander a concerned look, which he returned.

"Chief?" Lily asked as she answered the call.

Chief Aboye's voice was terse and grim. "Dawn, I'm afraid I have some bad news. There's been another murder, at another resort, about fifty miles away."

Lily's heart raced. No—another one? "And it's the same killer?" Lily dared to ask.

"I'm sending you all the details," Aboye said. "You two need to be ready. Now."

Lily nodded, and after taking a deep breath, she hung up the phone. She looked to Xander with a grim expression.

"There's been another murder," Lily said quietly.

"Son of a bitch," Xander said, hurrying up the hall.

CHAPTER TEN

He put his small plane in gear, setting it to take off out of the water, feeling so giddy inside. He'd done it—he'd claimed another victim, made another pose. And this one was so worth it.

The sea plane gained speed, then picked up into the air. The small plane glinted in the light, a sleek silver machine with a single propeller. Its wings, painted white, cut through the air as it lifted off the water's surface. A distinct humming sound filled the air as the plane ascended, a sound that reached a crescendo as it climbed higher and higher into the sky.

This plane had cost him a fortune, but it had been worth it. What good was money to him, anyway? He didn't need it. He needed to fly his plane more, to have unlimited access to all the different people he could across Florida. Florida, the Sunshine State—it was full of vanity, full of young, beautiful people who deserved to be put in their place.

And he'd done that. He'd left his victim in the most creative pose yet.

He had to try not to overexert himself with delight, otherwise he would get too hot beneath his layers, and that would make piloting the plane difficult.

The man closed his eyes, feeling the wind on his face as he soared across the ocean, with only the sound of the plane's humming to keep him company. The sun was hidden beneath thick clouds, but a streak of orange lit up the sky in front of him. He glanced down below and saw tiny ships and boats moving in a steady pattern.

He loved it up here, away from all his problems and worries. All that mattered was flying and finding new victims—and he had plenty of those in Florida. He smiled at this thought and kept going higher, until he felt like he was touching the sky itself.

And then suddenly it happened—a flock of seagulls flew past him in formation! They moved gracefully through the air, their wings flapping swiftly against each other as they soared alongside his plane. It was one of the most beautiful sights he'd ever seen!

He laughed out loud at how lucky he was to have had such an amazing experience. He felt so alive up here—the hum of the engine and rush of air around him made everything seem possible.

The man opened his eyes again and continued to soar over the ocean for what seemed like eternity, as if nothing else mattered anymore. The world looked different from above—more peaceful somehow—and for a moment, things felt good for him.

The horizon stretched out before him, seemingly never-ending—it was like looking into eternity itself. The clouds billowed ahead, forming shapes of animals and people as he flew closer to them. The flock of seagulls soared by, their wings flapping gracefully in unison with each other as they chirped happily at their newfound companion—the plane flying above them.

But the moment of euphoria was short-lived. Because as thrilled as he was by the last pose he'd made, by the last victim he'd claimed, he knew it wasn't over yet.

No… the thirst would come back. In fact, it already had. As he piloted the plane, he took out his sketchbook and set it on the dash, quickly drawing up an image of what his next pose might be—of who his next victim might be.

Another vain, self-centered man? Another narcissistic woman with no clothes?

Or perhaps it would be someone completely different this time. He smiled wickedly, savoring the possibilities. That was the fun of it—you never knew who your next victim might be.

The man continued to fly higher and higher, his mind spinning with anticipation as he thought about all the possibilities that lay ahead of him. It was like a game of cat-and-mouse, but one he intended to win every time.

This was the wake-up this state needed. Florida was full of far too many plastic people, and he intended to teach them all a lesson. Their beauty could not shield them. It was superficial. They were all as worthless with it as they were without it. It was society who had put value on something so vain, but he was there to remind the world that there was more to life.

In fact, he was helping. Doing a great service.

But he knew that was not something he could share with anyone. The secret had to stay between him and his victims.

As he neared the shoreline again, the man pulled his plane back into the air, flying over the crystal-blue water, the white sand, and the rolling green hills. He had to get back to his house—he knew this. His next victim was out there, waiting.

He could feel it.

Another fresh kill was on the horizon.

CHAPTER ELEVEN

The helicopter's rotary spun above as it flew Lily across the ocean—headed straight for Frannie Island, a tiny resort east off the coast, on a remote island. Lily couldn't believe it; now, it was certain that Roger wasn't the killer—not only was he dead, but a new body had just dropped, now off the coast.

So it was fair to say the killer didn't just travel by car.

The ocean spread before them as the sun descended toward the horizon. The sky above was a deep sapphire blue, gradually fading to a soft lavender as the sun spread its last rays of light across the water. As they got closer, waves rolled and crashed against the shoreline, stirring up sparkling foam that glittered in the setting light. A salty tang lingered in the air, mixed with the salty sea breeze and the sweet scent of tropical flowers. The evening was fragrant and calming, like a balm to the soul, and up ahead, Lily could see the lights from the resort brightening.

It would be dark soon, and they had no leads. As she gazed out at the horizon, Lily thought of her parents back in Aruba. This was supposed to be her first night staying with them in ten years… and here she was, on the hunt for a killer, a killer they knew next to nothing about.

Beside her in the helicopter, Xander shot Lily a reassuring look. "You doin' okay, darling?" he asked.

For once, Lily wasn't annoyed by his term of endearment—if anything, she was getting used to it. Maybe it just came with the southern boy package. "Fine, Agent Jackson," she said, keeping things formal. Unlike him, Lily did try to maintain some professionalism on a case. Xander was a good agent, but he was also a wildcard sometimes. Of course, the FBI knew and accepted that, so it wasn't Lily's place to pass judgment. He got results, and that was what mattered.

"Look at it this way," Xander said. "We lost another person, and that sure blows—but we have a chance here to make it right and catch the damn bastard doing this. So chin up. We've got this in the bag soon enough."

"I hope you're right," Lily said, "because so far, it's been pretty clear we're missing something major. The killer's trail seems to end with Roger. So what's next?"

"We just gotta keep goin,' that's all. We know it's someone local, someone with access to certain areas. We know it's someone who knows about the other victims and the way they died. So we'll just keep lookin', keep talkin' with people. Someone's gotta know something."

Lily was quiet as she looked below, watching the plumes of smoke rise from the resort's chimneys. She couldn't disagree with Xander—but she was still worried.

This case was taking a toll on her, and she didn't like it.

She couldn't help but feel that he was wrong. The killer had already gotten away—how did they have him in the bag?

The helicopter descended and flew over the resort. It was beautiful. The island looked like a slice of paradise. They landed on a flat piece of land near the beach and as Xander and Lily climbed out, they were greeted by a group of police officers.

Lily looked around. It was just about dark now, but they had set up a few torches by the beach, creating a makeshift camp. The warm glow of the torches illuminated the beach, and Lily saw that the resort didn't seem too far off. In fact, she could see the lights shining there.

"Agents Dawn and Jackson?" a young female cop said, coming over to them.

"That's right," Lily said, "and you are?"

"I'm Officer Lane Jenson—I was instructed to meet you here and take you right to the crime scene. We're facing a bit of an issue. This is a remote island and not all patrons have a way off, so we have a lot of confused and scared people at the resort. We've relocated them to their rooms, but we need to get this crime scene cleared up quick to avoid more of a frenzy."

"Oh, too bad for them," Xander said. "So they've gotta hide out in luxury for a bit. They'll be fine. We're not rushing our job."

Lily shot Xander a look. He was blunt, but also right. Still, Lily knew it was in the best interest of everyone to examine the scene and clear it out ASAP.

"Take us there, Officer," Lily said. "We'll make this quick."

Officer Lane nodded, and the three of them made their way toward the resort. The beach was beautiful; the warm sand glistened in the torchlight, and a cool breeze blew through Lily's hair. It was so peaceful, it felt like they were in another world. And yet even here, there was a murder.

As they arrived at the entrance to the resort, Lily noticed that it had been crafted with great care and attention to detail. There were lush gardens surrounding it, and there were bright flowers blooming from every corner. The building itself was an old-fashioned mansion made of white stone with intricate patterns carved into its walls. It seemed as if time had stood still here on this remote island. Everything felt untouched by modernity, but that was the aesthetic they were going for. There were officers milling about, and some employees being questioned, but Officer Lane was right—the guests had been cleared away. That was good. They didn't need too many eyes on them.

They followed Officer Lane down a hallway lined with large windows that revealed stunning views of the beachfront beyond them. They passed several doors until they came to an open restaurant area, one that reminded Lily eerily of where the last victim had been found. Here, there were more officers, and up ahead, on the patio, were camera flashes from the team collecting evidence.

In the middle of it all was a person sitting on a chair, wearing a sunhat. Lily expected to see long hair. A dress. Anything… female.

But as they got closer, Lily realized this wasn't a woman at all.

The victim was a man.

"What the hell?" Lily said, thinking out loud. Apparently Xander felt the same.

"We sure this is the same killer?" he asked.

Officer Lane led them right out to the patio. If Lily hadn't been sure it was the same killer before, she was sure now—the man was positioned on a chair just like the women had been, only his legs were crossed and his arm was positioned behind his head, as though he were just a live man relaxing and hanging out. But as Lily looked closer, she saw his face—completely devoid of life.

Her heart stalled.

The other women had different body positions—Grace had her hands crossed over her lap, while Veronica had been slouched in the chair like she had fallen asleep, although it was also clear the pose had been intentional. But this one felt even more deliberate, with the placement of the arm behind the man's head. Lily had seen many men sit like this before, in a relaxed, chilled-out pose.

But this man was dead. Her stomach roiled.

Lily stepped closer to the body, examining it carefully. She noticed the man's clothes were pristine, his white shirt open to show his toned stomach, like a normal beachgoer would look. His sandals were still on his feet, and there was no sign of struggle or injury on the body. She glanced up at Xander and Officer Lane for any clues, but they just shook their heads. There was no clear cause of death—no visible signs of trauma or injury to his body. Lily took a deep breath and tried to focus her attention on what she could see. She noted that he looked so calm and peaceful, it was almost like he hadn't been murdered at all—like he had just passed away quietly in his sleep.

But Lily knew that wasn't true. This man had been killed by someone with a purpose—someone who wanted to create an image with each victim, but why? That was the question that still eluded her, one that seemed impossible to answer without more evidence or more information about the killer's motives. For now, Lily could only examine what she could see from here—the perfect peace of death, and how it seemed so much different from life itself.

Who could have done something like this? Who would want this man dead? It seemed like the killer wanted everyone to know that they were here—but why? And if they didn't want anyone to know who they were or why they did it… then what kind of message were they trying to send? Lily had thought this was a gendered killing before, a man with a vendetta against women, but the addition of the male victim made this case even more unpredictable.

Lily turned to Officer Lane. "Do we have an ID?"

"Yes, his name is Jack Frenzy," Lane said. "Twenty-four. The girls at the restaurant knew him well. He's a regular here, apparently."

"Where are the witnesses?"

"Over there." Officer Lane pointed inside the restaurant, where three employees were speaking with two male officers.

Lily and Xander made their way inside the restaurant, weaving past the tables and chairs as they approached the witnesses. As they drew nearer, she could hear snippets of conversation—the employees had been talking about Jack with a sense of disbelief and sadness in their voices. As Lily and Xander reached them, one of the officers stepped forward.

"You're with the FBI?" he asked.

"That's right—Agents Dawn and Jackson," Lily said.

"These are the three that found him," he said, gesturing toward the girls. "We were just asking them a few questions."

The witnesses all looked at Lily and Xander with wide eyes, obviously shaken by what had happened. It was clear they were still trying to process everything, and it was only natural, given how unexpected this all was. "Do you know anything about why this happened?" Lily asked softly, her voice full of sympathy for what these people had gone through.

The witnesses glanced at each other before one of them spoke up. She was a young woman in her twenties with bright blue eyes and dark hair pulled back in a ponytail. "We don't know much," she said hesitantly. "Jack came here every day around noon—he always ordered the same thing, he liked to sit outside on the patio." She paused for a moment. "And he has so many friends, he's totally adored, so it was weird to see him here alone."

"Who found him?" Lily asked.

"We all kinda did," another girl, a redhead, spoke up. "Milly here has a crush on him so—"

"We went to go talk to him together," Milly, the brunette, cut in. "That was when we noticed he was, like… not moving!"

"He's always so lively," the redhead said. "So it was weird to see him like that."

"We tried to wake him up, but he wasn't responding," the redhead said. "So we called the police."

"And that's when we found out…" Milly trailed off.

Lily nodded. She knew they hadn't wanted to see what they saw. Their hearts were in the right place. They had done the right thing by calling the police and getting help. But they were also witnesses who needed to be questioned so they could figure out what had happened.

"Did you see anyone else here?" Lily asked. "Anyone suspicious?"

"It gets so busy in here," Milly said. "Like, so busy you can't even see straight and all you're thinking about is serving. But when we went to talk to Jack, we'd hit a lull in the traffic. None of us saw him come in…"

"Did you see anyone strange at all?" Lily asked.

The girls bit their lip and exchanged looks. Two of them shook their heads—but the third girl, a blonde, didn't.

"What about you?" Lily asked. The girl hadn't said much yet.

"I, well—" She took a breath. "It sounds crazy, but I could've sworn I saw someone weird earlier… not here, but out in the resort."

"Oh?" Lily said, leaning forward a little. Maybe this could be something.

"Yeah," the girl said. "I thought I saw a guy in… a winter coat."

"Here?" Xander asked, raising an eyebrow. "We're in Florida, ya know…"

"I know!" the girl said. "That's why it was weird. Maybe I imagined it."

But that was strange. Very strange. Lily thought back to the scarf she'd found on the beach by the last crime scene. That was also very strange.

So far, forensics had also found no fingerprints or anything on the bodies. The killer could be wearing gloves to hide his identity. Did he also wear other, heavier items? But he would boil to death out here.

"I probably imagined it," the girl said timidly.

"No, it's very helpful," Lily said. "We'll look into it."

"Thank you for your help," Xander said, and the officers led the witnesses back to their seats.

"So, a guy in a winter coat…" Xander said, as they walked around the restaurant. "And he's killing in Florida. Well, he's clearly not afraid of the heat."

"Or the sun," Lily said. "It's odd, though. I mean, this is still a beach resort. Don't people usually wear beachy clothes?"

"Yeah, it's not exactly winter in Florida, is it?" Xander said. "I guess we'll find out when we start asking around."

"I hope we do. It's going to be hard to find a man in a…" Lily trailed off.

"What?" Xander asked.

"This guy is already so far outside the norm," Lily said. "It would make sense if he chose to wear something that wasn't normal, don't you think?"

"Like a winter coat?"

"Exactly. But where would he get one around here? It's not like they sell them at the local store. And there's that scarf I found too."

Xander nodded. "Yeah, maybe your gut was spot on with that one."

Lily sighed. She hoped she was right. But maybe the blonde girl did just imagine it…

"Let's talk to the hotel staff," Lily said, "and see if they've seen anyone who matches that description."

CHAPTER TWELVE

The girl from the front desk looked up at Lily and fanned herself, sweat dripping down her face. "Oh god, I've never had to talk to the FBI before—this is a lot, oh my god!"

Lily and Xander had been trying to get her to settle down and talk for a minute now, but she was still in panic mode. Lily understood—someone had just been murdered—but it was hard not to lose patience when she really just needed information.

"It's all right, miss, you're not in trouble," Xander said. "We just need to pick your brain a bit and find out if you saw anyone suspicious."

"We're looking for someone in particular," Lily said. "A man—"

"Ah, sorry, this is just—" The girl fanned herself more, then leaned over the counter of the hotel's front desk, like she was about to collapse.

"You need an ambulance or somethin'? Damn," Xander said, visibly annoyed.

"No, no," the girl said, shaking her head. "I'm sorry, I'm just so—oh my god! Someone was killed here!"

Lily stepped forward and put a hand on the girl's shoulder. "It's okay," she said gently. "We know it's been a lot for you to process, but we need your help. Do you remember seeing anyone wearing something out of the ordinary? We're looking for someone in a winter coat."

The girl paused for a moment and seemed to think back over her memory.

"Hey," Lily said gently. "It's okay. We understand you're upset and we don't want to push too hard. We just need to know if you saw anyone who fits this description: a man wearing a long coat or some other type of heavy clothing? He would have stuck out from the crowd here."

The girl seemed to relax a bit at Lily's words. "Um… I mean, I don't think so? That sounds pretty weird… but I spend all my time in here for the most part."

"Is there anyone else who might know more?" Lily asked.

The girl nodded. "Yeah, there's this guy who works at the bar—he's a real character. Super friendly, knows everyone in town. He might have seen something."

Lily and Xander looked at each other. This could be the break they needed.

"Where is this bar?" Lily asked.

The girl pointed out the window. "It's by the pool out back. The police wanted us to stay near our positions, so he should be out there still."

Lily thanked her and they headed out, their steps quickening with anticipation as they made their way to the pool area. The sun was setting on the horizon, casting a deep red glow over everything around them.

As they approached the bar, they saw a man in his late twenties with shaggy blond hair leaning against the bar, talking to a couple of officers. They all looked over as Lily and Xander approached with their badges out. The bartender had a shocked look on his face.

"Whoa, the FBI is here? For real?" he said.

Lily nodded at the officers. "We can take it from here."

Tipping their hats, they left them alone with the bartender.

"This just gets crazier," the bartender raved. "I'm gonna need to tell the guys all about this!"

Lily couldn't help but glower. This guy seemed more like a frat brother than a bartender. She said, "This is a serious matter, Mr. …?"

"Oh, Josh Grayson!" he said, extending his hand to shake Lily's. When he offered it to Xander, Xander just gave him a look.

"You can shoot the shit with your buddies later," he said. "We've got a dead guy on our hands here and we need you to answer our questions."

"Oh, yeah, of course, man!" Josh said. "What can I help with? I've already told the cops everything I know…"

"We're looking for someone specific," Lily said. "We were told you have eyes on a lot of guests here, and we were wondering if you've seen anyone dressed strangely—such as in winter attire."

"Winter clothes out here?" Josh gaped. "You'd die in this heat, man!"

"Did you see somebody overdressed like that or not?" Xander cut in.

Lily shared his annoyance. They'd questioned a few staff by now, and still had no solid answers.

"Uh, not really winter stuff," Josh said. "But there is this one guy who stays here a lot… he's always wearing big fur coats with like, no clothes underneath. It's so weird. Some rich guy I think, he doesn't go out much…"

Lily and Xander exchanged glances. It seemed they had their man.

"Do you know what room he stays in?" Lily asked.

"It's always the same one," Josh replied. "The penthouse suite at the top floor—it's the only one up there."

Lily looked over her shoulder at the tall hotel rising into the darkening sky. All the guests had been told to stay in their rooms until the police could clear everything… so this guy—whoever he was—was likely up there at the top floor. Lily could see the lights were on.

"What's his name?" Lily asked.

"Marcus something… goes by Markie sometimes. He's a real popular dude, I think he spends a lot on the ladies, always ordering them drinks and stuff. Although now that I think about it, he does seem to always be on someone's tab… hmm…"

Lily nodded. They had what they needed—this Marcus guy could be exactly who they were looking for.

"Thanks, Mr. Grayson," Lily said. "We'll look into it."

They went to leave, but Josh said something else.

"Hey, I knew the guy… the one who died."

Lily looked back at him, and he was rubbing the back of his neck. "Jack was a really solid dude." Josh's face softened as he reminisced about his friend. "Jack was always so cool and calm, ya know? He was the kind of guy who would go out of his way for others without expecting anything in return. He'd give you the shirt off his back if you asked him to. I remember one time when a little kid got lost at the park, Jack spent hours looking for him until he found him safe and sound. Everyone just loved him—he had this infectious smile that could light up a room."

That seemed to be the case, Lily thought. The other employees seemed fond of Jack too.

"And then there was his sense of adventure," Josh continued with admiration. "He used to tell me stories about all the crazy places he'd been and things he'd seen. It sounded like something out of a movie! He even had some wild ideas to get us out of our dead-end jobs… it was like nothing could hold him back." Josh paused, smiling sadly as he remembered all the good times they shared.

It was touching to see how Jack had reached so many people, even the employees at the resort he was staying at.

"It really sucks that Jack is gone now," Josh said finally, shaking his head in disbelief. "He was an amazing person and an even better friend. Yeah, we didn't hang out outside of the resort, but still, he was a solid guy."

"I'm sorry for your loss," Lily said. "We'll find out what happened to him."

Lily and Xander thanked Josh again and headed toward the entrance of the resort. Once inside, Lily headed for the front desk, where the girl from earlier was still sitting, trembling. When she saw the FBI agents approaching again, she anxiously stood up.

"We need to know about a guest named Marcus who's staying on the top floor," Lily said.

"Oh—this, I can actually help with!" the girl said. She eagerly went onto her computer. "Marcus Wexner… yep, he's in the penthouse suite… has been for a long time."

"A long time?" Lily asked, her heart sinking. If Marcus had been here for the other murders, then he couldn't be their man.

"Yeah, a few weeks," she said. "He like, lives here. I think he even works remotely from here."

"Would it have been possible for him to leave the resort often?"

"Hmm, I don't see why not," the girl said. "There are lots of boat rides available for people to head back to the mainland if they need anything, although we try our best to keep the island well stocked."

Lily nodded. So it was completely possible that Marcus could've been staying here, and then gone to the mainland to commit the other murders, only to return.

"What do you make of this guy?" Xander asked.

"He's kind of, well…" The girl glanced over her shoulder. "Well, he can be a bit inappropriate with the staff. You know, the girls."

"Oh?" Lily asked in surprise.

“Yeah, he’s always asking us to come to his room and take care of him,” she said. “He even pays us for it, if you believe that! But I mean, it’s not like we would do it. He’s just really creepy. He always has these weird requests too.”

Xander said, “Like, what kind of requests?”

“Well, one time he asked for some of the female staff to dress up like a princess and a pirate and have a sword fight, and then he’d tell them what a great show it was,” the girl said. “Another time, he requested three girls in bikinis and then he’d have them have a pillow fight. The girls weren’t too happy about that. It’s not like any of us would ever do it. He always acts like he’s joking after, but we always find it super creepy.”

Lily and Xander exchanged glances, their suspicions growing. Marcus certainly seemed like he could fit the profile of a killer. He was an outsider, he had questionable requests, and he had been staying at the resort for quite some time. Lily could hardly believe what she was hearing. It was clear that Marcus had a taste for the macabre and enjoyed inflicting his own twisted sense of justice on those around him. This could indicate that he had an obsession with controlling others, which could lead to violent behavior. He certainly seemed to fit the profile of a serial killer, albeit one who preferred to carry out his deeds in a more subtle way than most.

The fact that he had been staying at the resort for weeks and was already known among the staff as being inappropriate and creepy only added to this suspicion. If he had been on the island for a few weeks, that also would have given him plenty of time to commit the other murders as well.

“Thank you,” Lily told the girl, “you’ve been a huge help. We’d better go have a chat with Marcus.”

The girl gave them a slight wave. “Good luck!”

Yeah. Lily was sure they might need it.

CHAPTER THIRTEEN

Lily and Xander made their way over to an elevator in the corner of the lobby. It seemed as if it could whisk them away to any floor in an instant. Lily pressed her finger against one of several buttons on its side panel, the top one, and then the elevator doors closed.

"Think this Marcus guy might pan out?" Xander asked, hands in the pockets of his jeans.

"I don't know," Lily said. "We know almost nothing about him, but he's definitely worth interviewing."

"I've been thinking about something…"

Lily looked up to see Xander had a hesitant expression on his face. His blond hair was slicked back, his eyes greener in the light of the elevator.

"What is it?" Lily asked.

"Something about the way he's been posing the bodies," Xander said. "Especially that last guy. It feels too deliberate. Think he's trying to make a statement?"

Lily's heart raced; she'd had the same thought earlier. She and Xander really were on the same wavelength often when it came to work. "I thought the same thing. It could definitely be a statement, I just don't know what. I mean, he's posing them to be in natural positions, like they're alive…"

Xander nodded. "It could be symbolic," he said. "Maybe he's trying to tell us something about life and death, or even his own personal views on the matter."

Lily thought it over for a moment, her mind racing. It seemed like the killer was trying to send some kind of message with the murders—but what? Perhaps he had a religious agenda, Lily thought. If that were the case, then maybe he was trying to make a statement about how humans should live their lives according to his beliefs. Or perhaps he was simply trying to get attention by making his victims appear as if they were still alive in order to shock people and gain notoriety. It could be anything really—but whatever it was, it seemed clear that this guy had no intention of slowing down his spree.

Lily trailed off, her mind racing. Maybe the killer was trying to show the victims as if they were still alive and well. Maybe this Marcus guy knew something about the victims that no one else did—something that could give them insight into his motives.

As they reached the top floor of the hotel, Lily took a deep breath and stepped out of the elevator, and the first thing she was greeted by was the sound of thumping music from just up the short hallway. This was the only suite on the top floor, so she knew it was coming from Marcus's room.

Not only that—but voices, like cheering, sounded.

"He having a party or something?" Xander asked, confused.

They made their way toward Marcus's room. Lily knocked, and it was only a few seconds before the door opened to reveal a huge party in full swing. Someone—a partygoer, presumably—had swung the door open and left without even checking to see who it was. Music played in the background, people were dancing and talking, and there was even a bar set up with someone serving drinks out of colorful glasses.

Lily stood stunned for a moment—had she come to the wrong place? This was all happening right on top of a crime scene. But then she spotted Marcus at the center of it all, his head thrown back in laughter as he chatted with some others around him, wearing a brown fur coat and no shirt underneath with only shorts on. He hadn't seen them yet. He was too busy having fun with everyone else.

"You think we should just walk right in?" Xander murmured in her ear, making her jump slightly—she hadn't realized he had been standing so near.

She took a deep breath and nodded firmly before stepping forward into the party. The chaos of it all swallowed them—there were people taking shots and egging each other on. The music was so loud, it pounded Lily's eardrums. As they tried to get through, it somehow seemed like there were even more people, and Lily lost sight of Marcus.

"So what do you think?" Xander asked her as they made their way through the sea of bodies. "Do you think this is how he does things? Throws these wild parties and then disappears for a few days before striking again?"

Lily shook her head slowly. It was possible—but right now, she wasn't sure what to make of it. She just knew that it seemed wrong somehow—like holding a party on top of a crime scene was some kind of twisted celebration of the killer's deeds.

"Where the hell is he?" Lily asked. With all the people dancing, it was getting disorienting, and the suite was massive.

"Let's split up," Xander suggested. "You take that side and I'll take this one, and we'll see if we can't find him."

Lily nodded and set off down the hallway, her eyes darting around as she searched for Marcus. She checked every room she passed, but he wasn't in any of them. He seemed to have completely disappeared. With a sigh, she returned to the main room where Xander was waiting with a concerned look on his face.

"I couldn't find him," he said, shaking his head. "He might have left while we were looking."

Lily frowned, feeling a wave of disappointment crash over her. They had come so close—but now it looked like they were out of luck when it came to finding Marcus before he could do any more damage or strike again. But he had to be here somewhere—he couldn't have gotten far.

Just as Lily was thinking they might need to check the hall, she spotted the fur coat ahead. Marcus looked back at them with a confused look on his face, and that was when Lily struck. She made her way straight for him, and once Marcus realized she was coming at him, he tried to run back, only to crash into another person, who shoved him away.

Marcus scrambled through the crowd, pushing people out of his way as he tried to make his escape. Lily followed close behind, determined to catch him. She chased him around the room, dodging dancers and drinkers alike as Marcus seemed to be heading for some sort of exit.

The two of them weaved between people who were either too drunk or too caught up in their own conversations to notice that someone was fleeing from the room. Neither of them paid attention to where they were going; all that mattered was getting away fast. The music seemed to get louder as they went, and for a moment Lily thought she lost sight of Marcus in the crowd—but then she spotted him again and kept chasing after him. Finally, a break in the crowd, and Marcus took off—but Lily was right behind him.

"Stop! FBI!" Lily shouted over the music.

Marcus looked back in horror, stumbling forward—crashing right into a snack table. A massive bowl of punch spilled all over Marcus and drenched his fur coat.

Lily was right on top of him and quickly cuffed him, huffing with exertion. Xander appeared beside her shortly after, panting heavily.

"You got him," he said in disbelief.

Lily nodded as she looked down at Marcus, who was staring up at her with a mix of shock and terror.

"What is going on here!?" Marcus exclaimed. "Who are you people?"

A small crowd of partiers had noticed and came over. A drunk woman slurred, "Oh my god, Marcus, is that even real fur?"

Now that she mentioned it, the way the punch caught on the fur of Marcus's coat looked more like the way synthetic fur reacted to liquid, not real fur. Marcus had a pale expression on his face as he looked around the room—as more and more partiers noticed he was being arrested.

But they didn't have his back, that much was clear. In fact, as Lily and Xander led Marcus toward the exit, the party simply parted and allowed them through. Once they reached the exit and went into the hallway, the door closed behind them—and the party continued without its host, as if he were never even there.

Once they were alone and away from the loud music, Marcus said, "What the hell is going on here? Who are you people?"

"We're with the FBI, shitbag," Xander said. "Care to tell us why you were running from us?"

Marcus was sweating. "I—I thought you were… I thought…"

"You thought what?" Lily challenged. "You were running from us because you know what you did, Marcus."

"I don't! I swear!"

Xander backed him against the wall. "You killed that guy down there, didn't you? And now you're having a big party to celebrate?"

Marcus shook his head. "No, I swear! Please, I didn't do anything wrong!" He rambled off excuses and explanations for why he was running, desperately trying to convince them that he was innocent. But Lily wasn't convinced—she knew that Marcus had done something wrong and was likely guilty of murder, but she wanted him to admit it himself.

"Save it," Xander sneered. "You were running from law enforcement and that's more than enough to tell us you're guilty of something. You're coming with us."

Lily looked down at Marcus and saw his whole body was trembling, his face pale and full of fear. She couldn't believe he was acting this way—he had just brutally killed a man and then thrown a party to celebrate it. She didn't see a shred of remorse on his face, but instead just fear.

"But I told you, I'm innocent!" Marcus insisted.

"You think we're just going to take your word for that, asshole?" Xander said.

Marcus took a deep breath and looked Lily in the eyes, his expression pleading. "Listen, I swear I had nothing to do with this. This is all a misunderstanding—a huge misunderstanding! I was just at the wrong place at the wrong time. I wasn't running from you guys—I was trying to get away from someone else who was chasing me. Some guy back in the alleyway."

Lily furrowed her brow, not sure if she should believe him. Marcus seemed desperate to prove himself and his story seemed plausible enough—but she still had her doubts.

"Just come willingly, and this can all be over," Lily said.

Marcus frowned and hung his head. It was clear that he knew the situation he was in—there was no way out, no matter how much he pleaded his innocence. He had been caught red-handed, and there was nothing he could do to change that now.

He allowed Lily and Xander to take him away, not uttering a single word as they marched down the hallway.

CHAPTER FOURTEEN

With Lily at his side, Xander stared down Marcus Wexner as he sat on the other side of the table in the interrogation room. The police station on the island was barely even that—it was more of an outpost (with a drunk tank), but it did have a tiny room fit for interrogating criminals. And Xander was pretty sure he was looking into the pleading brown eyes of one of them.

Xander had dealt with a lot of dirtbags in his career as an FBI agent—not all of them were killers, but he was damn sure almost all of them deserved jail time for something or another. Growing up in a trailer park in Texas, his… special interest in criminals had extended long before he'd realized he wanted to be in law enforcement.

But of all the kinds of lowlifes there were out there, the pleading, pathetic liars—those were the ones that ticked him off the most.

And that was exactly who Marcus Wexner was turning out to be. He was cuffed, but still wearing that ridiculous fur coat with nothing but shorts underneath, like he thought he was a real playboy or something.

However, before coming in, Xander and Lily had done some quick recon on "Marcus Wexner"—only to find there wasn't anyone with that name matching his appearance at all, not in Florida, not anywhere. Which meant it was a fake. They didn't want to admit that yet, though; they needed to work their way up.

"Please, you have to believe me," Marcus said. "I-I'm not who you think I am! I'm not a murderer, I have no idea what happened to the guy in the resort!"

"You were sure enjoying the occasion, though," Lily pointed out.

"A little too much," Xander agreed. He liked working with Lily. Even if this was only their third case, she was growing on him. He liked her fire and admired that she kept it professional. That wasn't his style, of course, but he could work with it. She balanced him out. He could be the loose cannon while she was the voice of reason. That dynamic was good for him.

"Look, I was just in the wrong place at the wrong time," Marcus pleaded. "I didn't kill anyone! I'm telling you the truth!"

Xander shook his head and sighed. "You were running from law enforcement when we found you, Marcus. That's more than enough to tell us you're guilty of something."

Lily raised an eyebrow. "What else do you have to say for yourself?"

Marcus looked up at them with desperation in his eyes. He was clearly trying to think of an excuse or a way out, but he knew it was hopeless. He finally shook his head again and said quietly, "Nothing… I don't know what else to say."

Xander leaned forward and narrowed his eyes. "Then why don't you start by telling us why you were running? What did you do?"

Marcus gulped and looked away before finally sighing heavily and admitting, "Look, I really am not who you think I am. I'm not even who I present myself as. All this stuff… the glamour… it's all a lie… look!" His eyes were pleading as he tried to show them his arm, but he was cuffed. "The fur on my jacket, it's not even real!"

"So what are you saying?" Lily asked.

"I'm a fraud!" he admitted. "I don't… I don't even have any money!"

Xander narrowed his eyes. Was he coming clean?

Marcus sulked in the chair. "I… this is what I do… I go to these resorts and I pretend to be rich so people will flock to me, and they don't even realize that they're the ones paying for everything. I rack up a huge bill with the resort, then I leave. Marcus Wexner isn't even my real name."

Well, this was a turn of events. Xander leaned back in the chair and crossed his arms with a whistle. "Well, well, well. So you admit it."

He blanched. "You knew?"

"Of course we knew," Lily cut in, learning forward. "We know Marcus Wexner isn't your real name. So who are you?"

Marcus sighed again and hung his head. He had been caught in his own web of lies, and he knew there was no way out. "My name is James Thomas. I'm a conman, and I've been running this scam for years."

Xander scoffed. In truth, this was making sense. But it sure as hell didn't clear him of the murders. This guy was a narcissistic lying conman—he could be a murderer too.

Lily looked him in the eye. “So why did you run from us?”

James sighed. “I saw you in the crowd and I panicked. I didn’t want you to know who I really was. I-I was afraid you’d start asking questions, and I didn’t want to explain everything. I was terrified you would find out that I was a fraud and then I’d get thrown in jail.”

Lily shook her head. “You really thought we’d arrest you for that?”

“I thought you would!” James insisted, but then he sighed and lowered his head, realizing how little sense his excuse made. “Look, I know it’s not… I know how it looks… but I never hurt anyone, I swear.”

“Only the people and businesses you’ve stolen thousands from,” Lily said.

“Well, so what!” James exclaimed, his expression twisting. “They’re all rich anyway! Those resorts make so much money, and all the tourists I meet are filthy rich! Who cares if I steal from them?”

“A real Robin Hood, aren’t you?” Xander sneered. He was getting sick of this fast. “Cut the shit, James, Marcus, or whatever the hell your name is. I don’t care about your stupid con. I wanna know why you killed Grace Maloney, Veronica Smith, and Jack Frenzy.”

“What?” James paled. “I told you, I didn’t kill anyone!”

Xander rose from his seat and slammed his fist on the desk. “Don’t lie to me! I know you did it. You had motive and opportunity for all three murders. And I’m sure if we search your room, there will be evidence linking you to the crime.”

James shrank in his chair, fear in his eyes. He stuttered, trying to come up with an excuse that would get him out of this jam, but nothing came out of his mouth except trembling words of desperation.

“You think you can just walk away from this?” Xander continued, poking James in the chest with a finger. “You think you can just take people’s money and murder innocent people without repercussions? Well, let me tell you something: justice will be served.”

“Agent Jackson,” Lily cut in, but Xander was on the warpath now—all he could see was red.

“You won’t get away with this, any of it,” Xander continued ranting. “We’re gonna book you so hard you’re gonna wish you’d just—”

“Jackson!” Lily shouted, cutting Xander off, and he looked back at her to see she was glaring at him. Looking down at James, he saw he was terrified.

Xander sighed. Damn it. Maybe that would've worked, but here Lily was, foiling his tactic. But the tension had already snapped like a rubber band, and it was too late to get it back up. Fine, then—they'd do it Lily's way.

He sat back down and shut up, letting Lily take over the interrogation, but he had to admit, he was a bit pissed. Xander knew he could be a cannon, but he got results.

Lily looked right at James and said, "James, can you tell us where you were last night and this morning?"

"Where else?" James said. "I was at the resort, hosting another party."

Xander's jaw tightened. If he had a party, there'd be a lot of witnesses who could corroborate his story… if he was at this resort when Veronica died, then he'd be cleared.

But that was only if his story was true.

James continued, "I had a big group of tourists last night and the staff can vouch for me. I'm sure they remember me." He paused to catch his breath before adding, "And then I had another event this morning. The guests were all from out of town and they still have their receipts from the event. They'll be able to confirm my alibi."

Xander's eyes narrowed as he looked at James. He was still skeptical, but there was something about his story that seemed plausible enough to believe it could be true.

"Can you give us a list of names we can talk to?" Lily asked.

"There was this girl, Jessie—she spent the whole night with me, doing, well… you know. She thought I was rich. There was Gary Phelps—he's a fat cat from Miami who came down to relax, and he's been there for two weeks, so he knows me well. And ask around the staff too, I know some of them will remember that I was ordering food and drinks all night!"

Damn it. Xander's jaw tightened. If all this was true, then his story would be too legit to say he was able to slip off to the mainland, drive to the resort in Ashlyn, kill and pose Veronica… no, it was looking less and less likely.

Lily nodded and said, "Alright, then, we'll talk to these guests and see if your story checks out." She stood from her chair and motioned for Xander to follow her out into the hallway.

"Wait, what will happen to me?!" James exclaimed.

Lily coldly looked over her shoulder at him as they reached the door. "We'll hand you off to the police, and they can investigate your apparent long string of thefts."

James sulked in the chair. "No… no…"

Well, Xander was at least happy James would get something coming to him.

Once Lily and Xander were outside the interrogation room, she turned to him and said, "You can't just barge in there like a bull in a China shop when we interrogate suspects, Jackson. Sometimes the full aggro tactic isn't the best move."

Xander couldn't help but feel his face heat up with annoyance. Partners or not, Lily was less experienced than him, and he'd been with the FBI way longer than she had. "Hey, don't forget your place, Lily," he said. "You're not my boss. We're partners. We make choices together, and you undermining me in front of a suspect in there—hell, that's enough to make me wanna call this in right now and tell the chief I'm not working with you."

Xander hadn't meant to say that much, but he couldn't help it—he didn't care if she was beautiful or a great agent or anything else, he felt disrespected and needed her to know it. He hoped she'd do the same if he made her feel that way on a case.

Lily glowered for a moment before she took a breath, taking it in. "You're right. I shouldn't have undermined you in front of the suspect, but I was worried you were getting too hotheaded."

"My being hotheaded has gotten me far in this industry," Xander pointed out, cooling off. "It's not always the right time and place, though, you're right. But we should always be on each other's sides, especially in front of perps."

Lily nodded. "You're right, Jackson. I'm sorry."

Feeling light again, he nudged her. "Nah, you're good. I'm sorry too. I was being a bit too hard, too soon."

"Maybe next time we should go in with more of a game plan on each of our roles," Lily said.

Xander smiled. "Yeah, sounds good."

They looked at each other before Xander felt the urge to make this right—he felt bad for getting frustrated with her, even if it was justified.

“Aw, hell,” he said. He opened his arms to see if she’d consent to a hug, and to his surprise, Lily managed a smile. She gave him a quick, one-armed hug, but he’d take it. He patted her on the back.

“We make a pretty great team, Dawn,” he said softly.

“We do,” Lily murmured, looking away. “No more bickering.”

He smiled. But now that that was out of the way, they had a bigger issue to deal with.

If James/Marcus wasn’t their guy, then someone else was, and it’d only be a matter of time before another body dropped.

CHAPTER FIFTEEN

Lily sighed deeply as she entered the hotel room, feeling like the stress of this case—and everything else—was going to cut a few years off her life.

They'd looked into James/Marcus's alibi, and it turned out he was telling the truth. People really had seen him around the time Veronica would've been abducted and killed, and so it was impossible for him to be the killer. He'd still be looking at prosecution for his crimes related to theft, but as for murder—he was clean.

That left Lily and Xander to accept the reality that their case had hit a dead end, and it was night now. They flew back to the mainland and found a hotel near West Palm Beach to spend the night in, because for now, they had no one else to investigate. No matching names of hotel guests, no forensic data extracted from any of the three bodies—nothing.

Lily entered the hotel room and was struck by its extravagance. The room was plush and luxurious, with a four-poster king-sized bed, covered in red and gold velvet. Walls of textured wallpaper and deep mahogany gave the room a warm, inviting feeling. A large flat-screen TV sat atop a wooden dresser, and the wide windows let in the glow of moonlight. Lily inhaled the heady scent of rosewood and sandalwood incense burning in the corner. There was also the sweet smell of freshly cut flowers, along with a subtle hint of citrus from a plate of fruit that had been left on a side table.

Lily didn't need all these extras, but it came with the area; this was a very rich end of Florida. But in truth, Lily would rather be spending this night back in Aruba, where she should have been.

Dumping her travel bag on the bed, Lily went over to the window and gazed up at the stars above the ocean view. The warmth of the moonlight mixing with the chill of the night air washed over her as she took in this moment. She wondered what her parents were doing, if they were looking up at the stars from the beaches of Aruba too.

She knew her father's health was declining; he'd seemed thinner than usual when she saw him, which still felt like a lifetime away, even though it was only this morning. She wondered how much time he had, if he'd ever give her any details…

The last ten years of her life without family had been hard, and sometimes Lily didn't realize that until she was alone. She'd buried herself in her work as an FBI agent, but she'd never been able to let anyone get too close. Even Eduardo, the guy she'd dated for the longest—he'd wanted to marry her, but Lily couldn't do it.

She couldn't bring herself to commit to him, because she was scared of letting anyone get too close. Too many people had left her life when she was a child, and Lily was afraid that if she let someone in, they'd do the same.

The thought made her heart heavy, and Lily realized that it wasn't just this case that had been weighing on her mind—it was all of it. She hadn't seen her family in so long, and even though it felt like a lifetime ago, the memories of them were still so vivid.

Lily's gaze drifted from the stars above to the stars beneath—the lights of West Palm Beach twinkling in the night sky as if they were calling out to her. She knew the answer lay somewhere down there—or maybe somewhere else entirely.

She was so used to being alone that the thought of having someone in her life, and what it would mean for her as a person—scared her. She'd been so focused on trying to fill the void with work, but now she was starting to realize that maybe there were other things she could do too.

But as Lily looked out at the night sky, she felt a longing for something more in her life. She wanted to be brave enough to open up, to find someone who could understand her and accept her for who she was—with all the baggage that came with it.

Lily pondered over her life and all its complexities. She'd come so far in such a short time, yet here she was—standing on the precipice between safety and something greater, unsure of which direction she should take.

Lily exhaled deeply as she looked out at the stars one last time, before turning away from the window and heading to bed. She sat down on the edge and took out her phone, but there were no messages, no one trying to reach her.

Looking at her phone reminded her—there was someone who'd reached out to her earlier.

Foster.

She knew Vincent Gould, the serial killer they'd locked away, couldn't get at them—he was in prison for the rest of his life—but hearing that twisted man was still thirsting for their blood made Lily uncomfortable, either way. Especially for Foster. He was an old man who lived alone—no wife, no kids, no family. In a lot of ways, he was like Lily. He was probably the closest thing she'd had to a father figure since her real family shunned her, and sometimes she wondered if she'd felt like a daughter to Foster too.

It was late, but now that she was alone and away from Xander's ears, Lily wanted to see if Foster could tell her anything else—even if it was just an update. She was feeling vulnerable and lonely, and she missed her old partner.

She dialed his number and let it ring a few times. Just as she thought he wasn't going to answer, his gruff voice came through the line.

"Dawn," he said.

"Foster." Lily's voice came out weak. "I just… I wanted to check in and see how you're doing. The Gould stuff freaked me out."

"Sorry if I bugged ya, kid," Foster said. "Just thought you should know."

"Well, he's a sick bastard. I'm glad you told me." Lily paused. "How… are you, Foster? How have you been since you retired from the FBI?"

Foster's voice grew softer, more relaxed. "Well, I can honestly say that retirement has been quite the journey. After leaving the Bureau, I decided to pursue my lifelong dream of traveling the world. I've been all over Europe, Africa, and even as far east as Japan! Everywhere I go, people are so warm and welcoming. It's really opened my eyes to how much beauty there is in this world. But I'm back in America now, settled down where I belong."

Lily smiled, feeling a wave of warmth rush over her. "That's really amazing, Foster. I'm glad you're getting to experience all these wonderful places. And it sounds like you've been able to find a place to call home."

Foster chuckled. "It took some time, but yes, I think I finally have. Though if anyone ever told me that I'd be living in Philly of all places, I wouldn't have believed them!"

"Philly?" Lily asked with surprise.

"Yeah, it's nice up here. What about you, Dawn? You still with that Eduardo guy?"

Lily's heart clenched. Sometimes when she thought of Eduardo, she did feel guilty. "No. Things got… too intense for me. I'm in Miami now, got relocated here, doing some work for both the US and the Caribbean."

"Wow, so you're pretty close to home then. You got a new partner down there?"

Lily laughed when she thought of Xander, the haughty, hot-headed southerner she'd been paired with. "Ex-Navy, ex-DEA, hot-headed Texas boy," Lily said with a chuckle. "Agent Xander Jackson. He's… something else."

"Well, I'm sure if anyone can handle him, it's you, kid," Foster said. "You two working a case right now?"

Lily's head spun just thinking about it. "Where would I even begin? We've got some guy killing tourists at different resorts, staging them in public places like they're still alive, only for unsuspecting staff to find them… two women and a man so far… no concrete suspects."

"Damn," Foster said. "That's some crazy shit if I've ever heard it. Wish I could be there to help you out, but you know I hung up my hat."

Lily sighed. "I know."

"But you're a sharp agent. You'll catch him. And for what it's worth, he sounds like a statement killer to me… try to figure out what he's saying with the bodies, and you just might find your man."

What he said made perfect sense. A statement… but what was it?

"And hey, I hope someday you can be happy with someone else too, Dawn," Foster said. All you need is to find the right person."

Lily frowned. "I… I hope you're right."

"When have I ever been wrong?" He laughed gruffly. "Anyway, it's late over here, kid. Call me if you need anything."

"Thanks, Foster. Take care."

The call ended, and Lily was alone once again. But she felt lighter now—talking to Foster always did have that effect on her. And what he'd said, about figuring out the message, that resonated with Lily. It was late, and she needed sleep, but she pulled her laptop out and set it up on her lap as she sat on the edge of the bed. She looked up the photos of each victim, then opened them up side by side.

First, they had Grace Maloney. The social media influencer. She was sitting poised, with her hands folded on her lap. Meanwhile, Veronica had been positioned like she was relaxing and staring out at the ocean. And Jack had been positioned like he was kicking back and having a conversation, with his hand behind his head and his leg crossed. All very natural, human sitting positions.

But what did they mean?

Lily's eyes were betraying her; she could barely keep them open.

She looked over the photos one more time and then closed her laptop. She was exhausted, but she had faith that in the morning she'd be able to piece together a plan. Tomorrow would be another day, another case—another chance to prove herself. But tonight, Lily allowed herself a moment of reprieve, just a few moments of peace while she pondered her life and everything it had become. She slid into bed and let out a deep breath. Her thoughts raced, but eventually they began to slow as she drifted off to sleep.

CHAPTER SIXTEEN

When Lily opened her eyes, she was in front of a stage.

A massive stage with its curtain down, and she was at the front row. She looked to her left to see Xander was beside her, and Foster on the other side. All around them, in the rows behind, were all the coworkers she'd had over the years; Chief Aboye, Chief Brock, all the FBI agents she'd ever worked alongside, filling row after row. They all stared up at the stage in anticipation, and their friendly chatter filled the room.

"Where are we?" Lily asked Xander, but he shushed her. Confused and panicked, she turned to Foster, but he just shook his head.

"Quiet, kid, the show's about to start."

Lily looked up at the stage. The lights dimmed around them, then lit up on the stage.

The curtain drew, then suddenly several bodies strung up like marionettes fell down. Lily gasped, her heart pounding. Each body had been placed in a different position, and they were all facing the audience.

"It's the statement," Xander whispered, "they've been arranged to form a message."

Lily looked closer at the bodies and noticed that each one was in a different position than the others. Grace Maloney was standing tall with her hands on her hips and her chin held high. Veronica was laid out with her arms spread wide as if she were embracing something. Jack had his arms crossed and his head tilted back as if he were looking up at something in awe. But they were dead. All of them. The crowd cheered and clapped as the bodies, like puppets, were controlled to move across the stage.

"We have to do something," Lily said. She tried to stand, but she was trapped. "We have to help them!"

"Relax, sweetheart, it's just a play," Xander said with a cruel smile.

Then, on stage, two more bodies dropped down.

Bile churned in Lily's gut. No—it was her parents, strung up like marionettes too, their eyes lifeless and dull.

"Mom! Dad!" Lily screamed.

The crowd hushed and all eyes were on her.

Realization flooded into Lily's veins, and she felt powerless to do anything as the show continued. Tears filled her eyes as she watched her parents being manipulated by an invisible force, their bodies jerking and twitching like puppets. The crowd laughed, but Lily could only stare in horror at the sight of her parents' lifeless bodies swaying on stage.

Lily wanted to jump up and save them, but something held her back—a strange force that kept her firmly rooted to the spot. She was helpless to do anything but watch as the play continued, her heart aching with every movement of their bodies.

But they couldn't hear her. The audience clapped and cheered as the bodies of Lily's parents were manipulated to move across the stage, arranged in a human tableau just like the others.

Lily felt sick, she wanted to run, but she couldn't move. She was frozen in place as tears streamed down her face, watching helplessly as her parents danced on strings controlled by an unseen force.

Then, a voice: "Now, for the finishing act!"

The crowd cheered. Lily watched in horror as another body dropped, strung up like a puppet.

Kara.

The puppet dangled there, rotating slowly.

And then, suddenly, the puppet began to move. Its limbs twitched and its head jerked up and down. The crowd gasped in surprise as the puppet's eyes snapped open and glowed with a brilliant blue light.

Kara was alive!

The strings that had held her still were now gone, replaced with an invisible force that allowed her to move freely across the stage. She moved gracefully, her movements more fluid than before. Kara smiled at Lily as she flew across the stage, spinning and twisting in ways that seemed impossible for a human body to do.

"Kara!" Lily screamed.

Then, Kara stopped. She seemed to hear her. She looked down at Lily—then, before Lily could react, Kara flew right at her, her eyes blazing in fury.

"No!"

Lily gasped for air and shot upright in her bed as a loud bang smacked against her door. Recovering from the dream, she looked around the room—she was in the hotel in West Palm Beach, and everything was the same.

Dream…

It was just a dream.

But it had felt so real, and the marionette-like vision of the bodies made Lily's skin crawl. It terrified her.

The banging on the door continued. She looked out the window—it was still dark, the sun not yet up, but she could see color rising on the horizon. It must've been five a.m.

"Dawn, you in there?" Xander's voice came through the door.

Lily sighed in relief—it was Xander. He must have heard her scream from the nightmare. She got out of bed, feeling a sense of calm wash over her as she opened the door to let him in.

"Hey," he said softly, his eyes searching hers for any sign of distress. "You okay?"

Lily nodded and gave him a small smile. "Yeah, I'm fine," she replied, trying to put on a brave face despite how shaken up she still was from the dream.

"I was coming to wake you up when I heard you screamin'," Xander said. "You sure you're okay, Lils?"

Hugging herself, Lily turned away. She was glad Xander had started calling her Lils as opposed to sweetheart.

"Just a bad dream," Lily said. "Don't worry about it."

"Well, all right," Xander said, and Lily was grateful he didn't push it. She noticed he had his laptop with him, and he moved past her to the table in the room. "Anyway, I wanted you up early because I had an epiphany. I was thinking more about the bodies and how they're placed…" He put his laptop on the table and opened it up, logging in. Lily came and stood beside him.

"I've been thinking the same thing," she said. "I just don't know what it means yet."

Xander nodded. "That's why I wanted to get you up early," he said, his fingers gliding across the keys as he pulled up the photos of the victims. "I think the killer might be a taxidermist."

Lily looked at him in confusion. "What?"

"The way the bodies are placed, it's almost like they're posed like a taxidermy animal," Xander explained. He went online and looked up taxidermy photos.

"You really think the killer is a taxidermist?" she asked, her heart racing at the thought of it.

Xander nodded slowly. "It makes sense," he said. "The way they position the bodies in their final resting places…it's almost like they're trying to preserve them." He pointed to one particular diagram of a deer head mounted on a wall, its glassy eyes staring out into nothingness. "That's how these people are ending up."

She hadn't considered that angle, but when he presented it like that—it was very plausible.

"Okay, I like your thinking," Lily said. "Maybe the victims visited a shop or something—maybe that's how he's choosing them."

Feeling excited, Lily grabbed her laptop from off her bed, then set it up next to Xander's. They both grabbed seats.

"You look up taxidermists in the area," Lily said, typing to log in. "I'm gonna check out the credit card information of all the victims and see if we can match them to a location that might have someone like that."

"Roger that," Xander said, and after Lily got dressed, they both delved into their work. Lily scrolled through the credit card information of the three victims, her heart racing with anticipation. She was hoping to find some sort of connection that would lead them to the killer. After a few minutes of searching, Lily was able to pull up the credit card histories for all three victims. She quickly scanned through them and was surprised to find that they had all visited the same museum in the past month. Intrigued, she looked over at Xander.

"Hey, Xander," she said. "Check this out—the three victims all went to the same museum at some point in the past month."

Xander leaned closer and peered at her laptop screen, his brow furrowed in concentration. "That's weird," he muttered. "What kind of museum? Some sort of history museum?"

Lily clicked on one of the entries and enlarged it so they could both get a better look at it.

She quickly searched the museum, finding out it was known for its taxidermy exhibits. Could this be where their killer was choosing his victims? Lily felt her heart rate increase as she shared her findings with Xander.

"It looks like it," she said. "The museum has a wide variety of taxidermied animals on display—dinosaurs and all that too—it could be a good place to find our guy." Lily nodded slowly, taking in this new information. If they were right, then it seemed like their killer was selecting his victims from people who visited this particular museum. It was a popular tourist spot, and located around the middle of all three resorts.

"Okay," Xander said, turning to his own laptop, "so we need to find the guy who deals with this exhibit."

He opened up his search engine and typed in the museum's name, followed by "taxidermist." After a few seconds, he clicked on the top result.

"Here we go," he said, pointing at the screen. "It looks like they have a full-time taxidermist on staff—a guy named Andrew Moore. We may have just found our guy."

Lily went on her laptop and into the FBI database. If Andrew Moore had ever been in the system, they'd know about it. After a few moments of searching, Lily finally found what they were looking for. "Bingo," she said, pointing at the screen. "Andrew Moore has a criminal record—attempted homicide."

Lily and Xander looked at each other in shock—could this be their killer? She quickly read through the details of the case. It was an old incident that had happened almost twenty years ago when Andrew was in his late teens. According to the report, he had gotten into a heated argument with someone in a bar and ended up stabbing him with a broken bottle. The victim survived, but Andrew Moore was arrested and sentenced to jail time.

He had served his time and kept out of trouble since then—until now. Lily felt sick to her stomach as she realized what they'd probably uncovered—the identity of their serial killer.

Xander frowned, his face grim. "Yeah, that's not good," he said. "He must be really desperate to go after these people." He shook his head and sighed. "We need to get down to this museum and find out what he's up to."

Lily nodded in agreement, her mind racing with ideas on how they could catch this man before anyone else got hurt.

CHAPTER SEVENTEEN

A plethora of tourists scurried through the halls of the museum, and Lily and Xander blended right in with them.

But Lily had never been to a place like this before. She'd been to many museums, sure, but this was different.

Lily's eyes lit up wide in awe as she looked around the museum's front hall. She had never seen such strange artifacts before, from ancient sculptures to exotic paintings to intricate tapestries. The walls were lined with ancient artifacts, some strange and unrecognizable, while others were familiar but out of place. Lily's eyes widened in wonder as she took in her surroundings, her gaze bouncing from one display to the next. She marveled at the mixture of ancient artifacts and modern pieces, the way the artwork seemed to come alive under the soft lights. Colors, shapes, and textures danced before her, captivating her with their stories and secrets. The museum was alive with the smell of antiquity. Dusty books and fragile parchment filled the air with a musty scent that whispered of secrets hidden deep within. There was also a faint smell of polish and wax, as if the museum had been recently cleaned.

And this was just the lobby. Lily could see why so many tourists came to this place—maybe it was a coincidence that all three victims had visited at some point recently, but something in Lily doubted that. The taxidermy angle was solid, and she had a feeling this Andrew Moore guy had a lot to answer for.

Lily and Xander made their way to the front desk, where several young people were working. Since the museum got so much traffic, it was well-staffed.

"I'd like to speak with the manager, please," Lily said to the employee. Subtly, to not alarm guests, she flashed her badge, as did Xander. The girl's eyes widened.

"Certainly," she said in a hesitant voice. She pointed toward a door at the end of the hall behind her. "He's through there. Just knock and he'll be with you shortly."

Lily thanked her before heading off in that direction, Xander close behind her. Despite their mounting suspicions, they were both filled with anticipation as they made their way down the hallway toward the manager's office. Whatever was waiting for them on the other side of that door could make or break this case—and potentially save countless lives in the process.

Lily knocked on the manager's door. Within seconds, a short, portly man opened it up, wearing glasses. His name tag read "Tom." "Can I help you?"

"Good morning, sir," Lily said, as she and Xander held up their badges. "Agent Lily Dawn with the FBI, and this is my partner, Agent Xander Jackson."

"Oh, dear," Tom said. "Is everything okay?"

"Actually, can we come in?" Lily asked.

Tom shuffled aside and allowed them into his office, which was a mess of paperwork. He had a figure of a pyramid on his desk, and what looked like several old scrolls on his wall. "What's going on?" Tom asked, flustered.

"We were hoping to talk to you about one of your employees, Andrew Moore?" Lily asked.

"Andrew? He deals with our taxidermy displays, mostly dinosaurs and all that. He's actually setting up a new exhibit right now. What about him?"

"We were hoping to have a little chat with him," Xander said. "He's a person of interest."

"For what?" Tom asked. "Andrew's a good guy, he wouldn't do anything illegal…"

"You sure about that?" Xander asked, lifting a brow.

"What my partner means," Lily cut in, "is that Andrew Moore has a criminal record. Did you know he was charged for attempted homicide in his youth?"

"What? No, of course not," Tom said.

Lily could see that Tom was genuinely surprised by this revelation, but she pressed on. "How long has Andrew been working for the museum?"

Tom thought for a moment before answering. "Well, Andrew started working here about seven years ago. He was highly recommended by a colleague of mine at the time, and I've never had any issues with him. In fact, he's been an exemplary employee—

always on time and willing to take on extra shifts when needed." Tom paused, seemingly lost in thought. "He's become quite knowledgeable about the museum's collection too," he continued with a smile. "Andrew knows all about our ancient artifacts and modern pieces—the way the artwork seems to come alive under the soft lights. He talks about the colors, shapes, and textures, captivating guests with their stories and secrets. He even volunteers to lead tours around the museum from time to time."

Tom chuckled fondly as if remembering something special from Andrew's past at the museum. "He even managed to get us some rare dinosaur bones that were featured in last year's exhibit," Tom said proudly.

"It sounds like you have a lot of faith in Andrew," Lily remarked.

"I do," Tom said firmly, meeting her gaze without hesitation. "In my opinion, there are far worse people out there than Andrew Moore."

"We understand he's setting up an exhibit right now," Lily said. "We'd like to take a look at it, if you don't mind."

Tom hesitated for a moment before finally nodding. "Yes, of course," he said. "I'll show you to the exhibit hall. But please be careful—it's still under construction."

He got up and opened his office door, beckoning for them to follow him. Lily and Xander followed close behind as Tom led them down a series of corridors until they reached the exhibit hall. It was immense, with walls lined with dozens of displays featuring intricate taxidermy pieces from all over the world. As Lily looked around in awe, she felt a thrill wash over her—if Andrew was capable of this, he could easily be capable of the murders too.

Tom turned back to them with a nervous smile on his face. "What do you think of the museum? Pretty impressive, right? It was founded twenty years ago, and I've been managing it for half that time. It's been quite a journey since then. We started off with just a few pieces, mostly donated by local collectors. But over the years, we've managed to acquire some of the most impressive artifacts you'll ever see. We've got ancient Egyptian mummies, medieval suits of armor, and even dinosaur bones from all corners of the world!"

Tom was clearly very enthusiastic about his work, Lily noted. He kept on speaking, as though it was a rehearsed speech:

"Visitors come from all over to see our exhibits—it's become one of the most popular attractions in town. And it's not just people who come here either—we get school groups from miles around too! All of them are eager to learn about history and culture through our collection. Of course, it hasn't been easy getting to where we are today. Every year brings its own challenges; new pieces have to be acquired, existing ones have to be maintained and repaired, and new exhibits need to be developed in order to keep up with the times. But somehow, we manage! I'm proud of this museum, and I'm proud of my staff for making it what it is today. Andrew has done so much for us—he's always willing to take on extra tasks and help out wherever he can. I couldn't ask for a better employee."

Lily nodded as she listened. Tom seemed very adamant on defending Andrew, and Lily was interested to see why. Did Andrew really come across as such a great guy?

"Sure, museum's great," Xander said. "But we're not here to sightsee, sir, so let's keep moving."

Shut down, Tom said, "Right, of course…"

Tom quickly led them to the back of the hall, where a large prehistoric exhibit was still under construction. It featured several lifelike models of dinosaurs and other animals from the era, along with interactive displays that provided visitors with information about each creature. Tom pointed out the various sections as they made their way through the area.

"We plan to open this up in a few weeks," he said. "It's been a lot of work, but I think it's going to be worth it."

Lily was amazed by what she saw—the attention to detail was remarkable. She could tell that Andrew had put his heart into creating this exhibit, and she couldn't help but admire his skill at bringing these ancient creatures back to life. As they continued exploring the exhibit, Tom explained some of the features they could expect when it opened, including interactive quizzes and puzzles designed to engage and educate visitors about prehistory.

"This is what Andrew's been working on," he said as they approached. "It's an interactive exhibit that takes visitors back in time to explore the era of dinosaurs. We'll be adding animatronic models, video displays, and interactive activities for children."

Tom stopped walking and turned back to Lily and Xander with a proud smile on his face. "What do you think? Impressive, isn't it?"

Lily nodded in awe at the sheer scale of the exhibit—it was clear that Andrew had put a lot of effort into creating this masterpiece. She could only imagine how incredible it would look once it was finished. But that was beside the point. They were here to catch a killer, not look at the sights.

Up ahead, a tall woolly mammoth figure took up nearly half of the room. The woolly mammoth was a large, imposing structure with its curved tusks reaching up to the high ceiling. Its fur was a mix of gray and brown, and its eyes were dark and soulful. There was some scaffolding set up around it, likely so Andrew could get up higher and make tweaks to the animal.

"Hmm, Andrew should be around here somewhere," Tom said, then called out, "Andrew, it's Tom, are you around?"

"Think he's hiding?" Xander asked.

"No, no, why would he hide?" Tom said. "I'm sure all of this is a misunderstanding. Tom, you in here?"

No response.

Lily took a few steps closer to the woolly mammoth, admiring its intricate details. She ran her fingers along its fur, marveling at how soft and lifelike it felt. Suddenly, she noticed a slight shift in the statue's posture, as if it were about to move. Lily stepped back in surprise, her pulse quickening as she realized she had disturbed something.

She squinted her eyes, trying to make sense of what she was seeing—and then it happened. The woolly mammoth toppled right down toward her.

CHAPTER EIGHTEEN

Lily felt a strong force shove her from the side, tackling her away as the mammoth fell onto the ground, its massive frame crinkling and breaking where it landed. Lily's heart raced as she realized Xander had shoved her out of the way—and she was now staring right at the thing that would've crushed her enough to do some serious damage.

On instinct, she looked to see if Tom, the manager, was okay—and he was standing back, his eyes wide as he looked down at the wreckage of the beast.

Then, up in the scaffolding, there was a man. He looked down at them with wide eyes.

"Oh my goodness, folks, are you okay?!" he said, rushing down the stairs of the scaffolding.

It was Andrew Moore, in the flesh. He looked like a normal person—brown hair and eyes, a face you wouldn't look twice at on the street. The only mugshot of him in the system was from his youth, but he was older now, his face with deep-set lines. Was this their killer?

Before Lily could react further, Xander stormed away from her and right at Andrew.

"You son of a bitch!" Xander shouted, going right up to Andrew as he reached the ground level. Andrew backed up, holding his hands up. "Were you trying to goddamn kill us?" Xander demanded.

"No—it was an accident, I swear!" Andrew insisted.

"An accident, my ass," Xander spat. "You knocked the mammoth over on purpose! What the hell were you thinking?"

Andrew looked around frantically, his eyes darting from side to side as he tried to come up with an explanation. But Xander wasn't buying it—and neither was Lily.

"You knew we were here," Xander said, "you knew that lady was there!" He pointed at Lily. "You knocked the mammoth over on purpose!" Xander yelled, pointing an accusing finger at Andrew. "You tried to kill her!"

But Andrew shook his head vigorously, his hands still held up in protest. "No, no! I swear it was an accident," he said, desperation in his voice. "I had been working on the mammoth all morning and I guess I just didn't notice anyone else was here. But I would never try to hurt anyone—you have to believe me!"

Tom stepped forward then and placed a calming hand on Xander's shoulder. "Let's not jump to any conclusions," he said calmly. He looked at Andrew with an expression of understanding. "Andrew has been with us for years now—he wouldn't do anything like this intentionally." He patted Xander's shoulder as if to reassure him that everything was okay and that Andrew was innocent of any wrongdoing.

Xander seemed to relax somewhat, although Lily could still see the anger burning in his eyes as he stared at Andrew. Tom continued on, trying to defuse the situation before things got worse.

"Now let's just take a step back and think about this logically," Tom said softly. "We don't know how this happened or why it did—but we do know that Andrew is a good man who wouldn't do anything to hurt anyone willfully or recklessly."

"Are you joking me, Mr. Manager?" Xander said, then flashed his FBI badge in Andrew's face. Andrew's eyes widened more, and Lily knew it was her time to step in. She came over too, also holding up her badge.

"Andrew Moore," Lily said. "We're with the FBI. We're here to ask you a few questions."

"What about?" Andrew asked. "I swear, I didn't knock the mammoth over on purpose."

"Bullshit," Xander snapped.

But Lily was over the mammoth. She just wanted to get to the bottom of everything else, and if Andrew was their killer, then they needed to prove that.

"Can you come down to the station with us?" Lily asked.

Andrew hesitated. "But… I'm working right now…"

"It's okay, Andrew," Tom said. "It's better if you get this cleared up."

But Andrew still looked nervous. Lily was afraid he'd start to run, but he just kept standing there, fidgeting. "Can you at least tell me what it's about?"

"You really wanna know?" Xander said. "Fine. We're looking into three murders, and based on all your creepy taxidermy shit here, we think you might be the guy we're looking for."

"Murder?" Andrew gaped. "I'd never do that!"

"You attempted it before, remember?" Xander taunted, and Andrew's face fell. He looked at the floor.

"So it's true?" Tom asked.

Andrew sighed. "I was always worried this would come back to haunt me… it's true, I had an altercation when I was young, and I nearly killed someone. But thank God, it was unsuccessful. I've been trying to atone for it all my life."

He looked up at them, his eyes pleading. "I'm not that person anymore. I would never hurt someone intentionally—you have to believe me!" he said earnestly. "I've never even been in a fight since then! I just can't understand how this happened… You have to believe me," he said. "I'm innocent of these murders. I've been trying to make the world a better place since that day—and now, I'm here helping people find solace and peace through taxidermy. I would never hurt anyone again."

He seemed sincere enough, but Lily had met a lot of guilty bastards who seemed nice and sincere at first. He wouldn't be getting off the hook that easily.

"That's very nice, Mr. Moore," Lily said, "but we still need you to come with us and answer some questions."

Andrew looked around at the mess he had created and sighed. "I guess I don't have a choice," he said. But Lily could see the hesitation in his eyes—he was trying to find an excuse not to go with them. He seemed to realize this as well, and he quickly added, "But could you at least give me a few minutes to clean up this mess? It wouldn't take long."

"Quit looking for an excuse to stall us," Xander snapped, not having any of it. "You're coming with us. Now."

Lily put a hand on Xander's shoulder and gave him a look. Then she turned to Andrew, her voice softer. "We understand your reluctance," she said gently, "but it's important that we get to the bottom of this as soon as possible. We promise that this won't take too long, and you'll be able to come back here when we're done."

She glanced at Tom, who nodded in agreement. With that assurance, Andrew seemed to relax a little bit. He nodded slowly and said, “Alright then. Let’s go.”

***

They took Andrew down to the nearest police station, who let them take over the interrogation room without hesitation. Lily knew they had no evidence Andrew was guilty right now, so they could’ve interrogated him anywhere, but the police station setting often put perps on edge, and on edge was where she wanted him if he was guilty. She wanted him to feel like he’d already been caught, and then he’d be more likely to fess up.

If he was guilty.

Now settled into the interrogation room, Lily and Xander sat across from Andrew Moore. They’d gone over their game plan together; Lily would play nice, while Xander would be the hard ass, but Lily asked him explicitly to control his temper. Andrew had a mild temperament and she didn’t want to freak him out and make him clam up entirely. Too much aggression could cause him to go catatonic, and Lily wanted him talking.

“So, Andrew,” Lily said. “We’ve already told you why you’re really here. I’m going to show you three photos now, and I’d like you to tell me what you see.”

Andrew swallowed and nodded. Lily took out the pictures of the three victims. Grace, posed on a chair with her hands folded. Veronica, like she was slouching. Jack, like he was hanging out.

Andrew looked at the pictures. “These people are…dead?” His face was pale.

“They are,” Lily said. “What do you think about these pictures?”

“Well… the first thing I notice is the way they’re all sitting… they were found like this?”

Lily and Xander exchanged a look. Xander kept quiet, letting this go on.

“They were,” Lily said. “What about the posing stands out to you?”

Andrew adjusted his glasses and took a closer look. “It looks… staged,” he said.

“You can tell that just by looking at these, huh?” Xander said suspiciously.

"Well, it's a guess," Andrew said. "No one just dies like that, with the exception of maybe the middle woman." That would be Veronica.

"Her staging was deliberate too," Lily said.

"All right," Xander said, sighing, "let's cut the crap, Andrew. I think you know why these people are staged like this. I think you staged them like that yourself. Maybe it was another one of your strange little exhibits, huh?"

"What? No!" Andrew blanched. "I'm innocent," he insisted. "I don't understand what's going on here, and I would never hurt anyone. I don't even know these people!" He looked between the two of them, pleading for them to believe him.

"Bullshit," Xander said. "You know all about these people."

"But it's true!" Andrew insisted, his voice rising in desperation. "I didn't do this! I would never hurt anyone like that. I'm an artist, not a murderer!" He slammed his fist on the table in frustration. "You have to believe me!"

Lily and Xander exchanged another look. She could tell he still wasn't convinced, but Lily was starting to think Andrew might be telling the truth after all. He seemed so docile…

"Hey!" Xander shouted. "Don't raise your goddamn voice at us. We're the ones asking the questions here, so learn your place, Mr. Moore."

Andrew deflated in his chair. "Sorry. I'm sorry. It's just, I want to re-create life, not take it away. As you could see in my prehistoric exhibit, I put that woolly mammoth together myself…"

"You're very talented," Lily said, sitting upright. "You would easily be able to place these people in these positions."

"But I didn't," Andrew insisted. "Please, you have to believe me."

"Where were you yesterday morning, Andrew?" Lily asked. It was time to get the facts. "And yesterday afternoon, as well?"

Andrew sighed and slumped in his chair. "Yesterday morning, I was at home," he began. "I had taken the day off from work, and I was just…relaxing. I slept in late, then got up around noon to make breakfast for myself. After that, I showered and decided to go for a walk around the park nearby. It was such a beautiful day outside, the sun was shining and there were birds chirping everywhere." He smiled wistfully as he remembered the peacefulness of it all. "I must have been walking for about an hour before I made my way back home. Then I had some lunch, watched a movie, and then just sort of lounged around until dinner time."

"And you live alone?" Lily asked.

"Well, yes," Andrew said. "I'm a bit of a lone wolf…"

"And let me guess, no one saw you yesterday when you were out on your little walk?" Xander asked. "You talk to any neighbors? See anyone who can corroborate that story?"

The reality seemed to dawn on Andrew. "Well… no, it was a quiet day, but…"

Xander shook his head and began to laugh. "You expect us to believe that?" he asked. "Your little alibi is about as thin as tissue paper, Andrew. It sounds like you were just trying to cover your tracks here."

Andrew's face paled as he realized his story had only served to make Xander more suspicious. "No, I swear it's the truth!" he said desperately. "I didn't do anything! You have to believe me!"

"You expect us to believe that you were out for a leisurely stroll and no one saw you?" He shook his head in disbelief. "Do you think we're stupid? That's an awfully convenient alibi."

Andrew gulped, fear pooling in his eyes. He had been so sure that the two of them would believe him, but now it seemed like they were accusing him of lying. He stuttered out a few words before finally giving up and burying his face into his hands dejectedly.

"I can't believe this," he murmured. "Why won't you believe me? I'm telling the truth!"

Xander snorted and shook his head. "Nice try, Andrew. You're going to have to do better than that if you want us to believe your alibi." He crossed his arms and leaned back in his chair, a satisfied smirk on his face. "I think it's time you start telling the truth around here," he said sternly.

Andrew gulped and shifted nervously in his seat. But Lily—she wasn't so convinced. It was possible Andrew was being honest. A thought occurred to Lily; it was strange, how the killer had been able to get each body into the restaurants without being seen. He'd been able to set them up, seemingly surrounded by people. How could no one notice that? How did he get the bodies in there, anyway?

She needed to do more… examine the grounds of each resort. Maybe that would give her a clue as to how this person was skulking around like that. Maybe Andrew was their guy, and she knew Xander wouldn't let it drop so easily. But Lily had an inkling in her gut that there was something she'd missed.

She stood up. "Andrew, Agent Jackson will continue to take care of you," Lily said.

"What? Don't leave me here with him!" Andrew exclaimed.

Lily gave Xander a look—to remind him not to lose his cool, and he just nodded. He seemed to get Lily had a reason for wanting to leave.

With that, Lily left the room—she had more digging to do.

CHAPTER NINETEEN

Set up with her laptop in the briefing room at the West Palm Beach police station, Lily searched for footage of the resort grounds. She'd quickly called Chief Aboye and requested that they get blueprints sent to them, but they hadn't come through yet. Until then, Lily was looking up footage from the resorts. All three of them had drone footage used in advertisements that showed almost everything from a bird's-eye view, so Lily started with the Ashlyn resort, as that was the first resort she'd gone to, even though Veronica was technically the second victim.

The footage was beautiful, showing the lush gardens and the pristine beach. The resort truly could have been a paradise, if not for the tragedy that had occurred there. Lily watched as the drone moved over the pool area and then zoomed in on one of the restaurants. It was here that the second body had been found; it looked so peaceful now, with no sign of what had happened there, with people in the video laughing and talking.

Then Lily noticed something. At one table, an employee wheeled a cart, covered in a white cloth, toward the customers, covered in food. A food and drink trolley… there were many of them.

The realization hit Lily like a ton of bricks. The killer must have been using these trolleys to move the bodies around! It made sense—the trolleys were large enough to hide a body, and could easily be wheeled around without being noticed. Plus, the trolleys were frequently used by resort staff, so it was easier for the killer to blend in with the crowd and not draw attention.

Lily felt her heart racing. If she was right, then this could be the clue that she needed to catch this person once and for all. She just had to prove it. But how? This theory on how he moved the bodies around didn't exactly reveal anything about who he was… and that hint about the winter coat… that still seemed the most relevant to Lily. Could he be a staff member? No, that wouldn't make sense… he was at three different resorts, and there was obviously no way he could be employed at all of them.

Lily leaned back in her chair. She was no closer to figuring out who the killer was, despite having a better sense of how he moved around. All she had were theories, but no real evidence. She'd have to go back to the drawing board and come up with more ideas. Lily sighed in frustration. She felt so close to the answer, but still did not have enough evidence to make any sort of real conclusion.

She just needed one more clue, one final piece of information that would help her solve this case and bring justice to Veronica and all the other victims. All Lily could do now was keep searching, and hope that eventually something would turn up.

Her mind kept going back to the winter jacket and scarf. Maybe it was a coincidence someone had been seen wearing a winter coat at the last resort, and that Lily found a strange scarf in Ashlyn… but that still seemed like the strangest potential clue of all…

Were they looking for a chronically cold person? Someone with a condition that made them want to wear so many layers in hot weather? But even then, if the coat person had been sneaking in and placing the bodies, even with a trolley, he would've had to change into some sort of disguise. Staff and patrons would've noticed a man wearing that many layers, and so far only one eyewitness had caught a glimpse of him.

Hmm…

What if it wasn't that the person was cold…

Why else would someone cover themselves up?

Lily thought on it, her mind going over the details. Maybe he wasn't cold, but trying to hide himself from the world.

Was he insecure?

Did he have some sort of personal trauma that caused him to try and cover up his face?

Lily knew she was on to something. She began searching through databases and records, trying to find out if anyone with a history of mental health issues had been seen around the resorts at the time of the murders. It was a long shot, but it seemed worth a try. Lily came up with no real conclusions though and realized trying to find him this way was like trying to find the proverbial needle in a haystack. She went back to his psyche, to see if she could build a more concrete profile.

Why else would he cover up?

Was he embarrassed by his identity?

Maybe he thought he was ugly, and that's why he kept himself covered up? But then again, if that was the case, why would he be so bold to commit murder at a public place like this? It didn't make sense.

Lily shook her head, realizing she was getting nowhere with this. She needed more information, something concrete she could use to track him down. With a sigh of frustration, Lily grabbed her laptop and started searching for any other clues she might have missed. She had to find out who this killer was before anyone else became another victim.

Did he have something to hide, something that would make him stand out in any way?

Maybe he had a birthmark, or a scar. It would explain why he was so careful to cover himself up and not draw attention.

It could also be possible that the killer had some sort of deformity or disfigurement that made him want to hide from the world. Or maybe he was simply paranoid about being seen by anyone, so he covered his face and body with heavy clothing wherever he went. Yes, maybe it was something much deeper than feeling "ugly" or "insecure."

Lily was onto something here—she could feel it. She decided to turn back to the victims, to see what might draw them all together, based on the profile she was building of the killer.

Grace, Veronica, and Jack—they were all conventionally beautiful people. Young, athletic, and near flawless when it came to their physical appearances.

Flawless…

Beauty…

Was that what this was all about? Revenge on the beautiful?

The perfect crime.

Lily thought back to the winter coat and scarf—was the killer trying to hide his identity due to a feeling of inferiority when it came to physical appearance? Was he targeting people who were better looking than him?

Lily felt a chill run down her spine as she realized what this could mean. Could it be that this killer was out for revenge on the good-looking people of the world? That he was targeting those he deemed too beautiful, too perfect? It seemed far-fetched, but in a twisted way, it made sense.

It was possible that the killer had been wronged in some way by someone they perceived as more attractive than themselves, and they were now taking out their anger on others who fit that description. It

would explain why they chose to target these particular victims—they weren't randomly chosen; each one had something in common that drew them together: their beauty.

Lily knew she had to find out who this person was soon before anyone else fell victim to their twisted desires. She decided to search through police records once again, trying to see if any past crimes related to this kind of behavior had ever been reported or documented anywhere. If she could track down any potential suspects with similar motives or backgrounds, then maybe she'd be able to get closer to solving this case and finding justice for the victims of these brutal murders. When she didn't immediately get a hit, Lily realized this was a two-person job—if she was right, then Andrew Moore didn't fit the profile. He was average-looking, maybe even good-looking to some, and Lily felt it in her gut that they were looking for someone a lot more twisted than him.

She rushed out of the briefing room and hurried through the hall of the station to the interrogation room. She knocked once and poked her head in to see Xander sitting there with Andrew. They looked over at her.

"Jackson," Lily said to Xander. "We need to talk."

***

"So you think he's what, disfigured?" Xander asked Lily after she'd explained the theory. They were standing in the briefing room now, and Lily just hoped Xander would take her seriously.

"Yes, I think he's targeting beautiful people and covering himself up in heavy winter clothes to hide his disfigurement," Lily said.

Xander crossed his arms, his brows pinching as he thought on it. "I hope you're right, Dawn. Moore was talking about getting a lawyer so I had to let him go after you pulled me outta there. Maybe you could've kept him away from that."

"I'm sorry, but I had to follow my gut here," Lily said. "If I'm right, then Andrew doesn't fit the profile, and we have no physical evidence on him. We should look up any guests at any of the resorts who might suffer from some sort of physical condition or illness, and go talk to them."

Xander sighed, but he nodded in agreement. "Let's do it," he said. "If we can stop this person before anyone else gets hurt, I'm all for it."

Lily smiled in relief. "Thanks, Xander." She knew she couldn't do this alone—she needed someone with the same determination as she had to get to the bottom of this case.

Setting up their respective laptops, they sat at the table and combed through guest lists, cross-referencing them with police reports and medical records. There were a lot of people, and none stood out so far who also had criminal records, so Lily focused on medical records.

Then she found it—a burn victim who had checked into the Ashlyn resort a few weeks before the murders began, named Henry Perry. She clicked on the file, and her heart skipped a beat when she saw his photo. He fit the profile perfectly—his face was scarred from burns, and he looked deeply unhappy and disturbed in his passport photo. His hair was matted and his eyes were the eyes of a man who lived in eternal pain. Moreover, when she looked at Henry's credit card information, she noticed he'd checked into a different hotel not far from the Ashlyn resort, even though his address was registered to West Palm Beach. This guy came from money—his parents had died in the fire that disfigured him when he was seven, and he was left a handsome fortune he was given access to when he turned eighteen. He was currently thirty-two years old.

"I think I have a potential," Lily said.

"Me too," Xander said. Lily checked his screen—a man with a facial deformity looked back at her from the screen. "His name's Augustus Child, he's currently staying at the resort Veronica was found dead at in Ashlyn. He's from New York, but he's been staying here for a few weeks on a honeymoon with his wife."

"Pretty long honeymoon," Lily commented. She wasn't sure a man with a wife was who they were looking for. "I think we're looking for more of a loner type, but he's worth talking to."

"Agreed," Xander said.

Lily shut her laptop and stood up. "We're gonna have to split up then—we need to get some ground covered, because at this rate, more bodies will drop today."

Xander rose from his seat and nodded. "Let's do it," he said, determination in his voice. "We'll find this guy and make sure he doesn't hurt anyone else."

CHAPTER TWENTY

This stupid, stupid woman.

She had no idea what was coming for her.

As he pushed the cart, he kept his head low and smiled, making his way through the busy hotel lobby. He hadn't found the time to get his disguise yet, but that was okay for now—first, he had to take his victim, then he would go back to the room to prepare her. Then he would break into the supply closet and find an outfit to wear as he wheeled her out to the restaurant patio to create the show for all to see.

At this point, he'd done this so many times, he had it down to a science. The only thing that had gone awry with this location was that he'd actually had to use his card to rent out a room. Usually, he would steal one and sneak in, or pay someone else to do it for him. But the hotel staff had noticed him, and he'd had no choice but to rent a room to not seem suspicious.

It would all be fine, though. He would quickly place the body, go back for his belongings, and wipe the room clean. He'd be gone before they noticed. It wasn't like anyone ever really saw him, anyway. He was invisible.

But not for long. For this woman he was stalking—he'd be the last face she ever saw.

She was strutting up ahead, looking down at her phone, wearing a skimpy dress—so oblivious to the world around her. So vain. So foolish.

He felt a surge of rage course through him as he watched her. How dare she think she was so much better than everyone else, when she was nothing special? She was nothing but a waste of life.

But he'd show her. He'd make sure she paid for it. He'd make sure everyone knew what happened when someone lived like that—when someone thought they were better than the rest of us.

He began to increase his speed, tightening his grip on the cart as he moved closer and closer toward her. Soon enough, they would be one and the same—she would be gone and forgotten, while he would have made his mark in history forevermore.

He felt his anger rising. He thought about her body, how it would soon be positioned like a mannequin, and how he would make sure everyone saw it—everyone who'd judged him or laughed at him or looked away when he walked by. This was his art; his revenge.

People like her didn't understand what they still had. Beauty. Not just that—but family. He'd lost his parents so long ago that they felt like mere memories. He'd been tossed through the foster system until he was eighteen, when he finally got the money that was rightfully his.

But no amount of money could change the fact that he had endured years of abuse from other children and foster families alike. They would point and laugh at his burns, call him terrible names.

He thought of the relentless taunts, the cruel jibes. They had no idea what it was like—they'd never felt pain like he had. He was alone in this world, and they were too blind to see it. He thought about the foster parents who'd treated him like a dog. He thought about the foster siblings who'd tried to peek at his scars, who'd called him a freak.

He thought of the little girl who'd tripped him in the schoolyard, and the cruel kids who'd made fun of him—even the teachers who'd ignored his pleas to be left alone.

He thought about the kids singing in the locker room, the ones who'd called him a monster.

They had no idea what it was like to go through what he had.

How he'd lost his parents when he was so young, left behind in this world with scars. Every time he looked in the mirror, he heard their screams. Every time he looked in the mirror, he was reminded of how the world had tortured him after.

He didn't deserve it. He was a child who deserved love, but he'd been deemed too ugly, and now he hated all things to do with beauty. Money? It didn't matter. The only thing that got people ahead in life was their worthless beauty, but it all would fade someday anyway, and they would all end up as ugly and alone and dead as him.

He thought of his parents, the only people who had ever truly loved him. He wished he could have them back, even for a day. He wished he could tell them how much pain he'd gone through in their absence. He thought of all the memories they'd shared, like family trips to the beach or camping in the forest or playing catch in the backyard. He remembered how his dad used to put him on his shoulders so he could see farther than everyone else, so he could see above it all.

He wished for one more hug from them, one more reminder that they were there no matter what happened—even if they weren't physically there with him anymore.

His heart ached with sadness that quickly burned into fiery anger. Wishing didn't do anything. All he could do was move forward and live with the pain he'd been dealt. It was something nobody else would ever understand—least of all her.

The world was cruel, and it needed to pay for its crimes. His art would be the only way to make that happen.

He looked at the woman, who was still aimlessly scrolling through her phone as she walked. Oblivious. Vain. People like her were the ones who had tormented him. Beautiful people… normal people…

But soon enough, they would see it. They would understand who he really was underneath all the scars and all the anger—they would know his truth and his power.

He had wanted to be loved, but instead he was forgotten. He was invisible.

But soon enough, she wouldn't be the only one who would remember his name. Everyone would know it—and remember what happened when someone crossed him. His revenge was coming—and there was nothing anyone could do to stop it.

They would all pay.

And then they would see what really mattered in this world.

CHAPTER TWENTY ONE

Lily's heart pounded as Xander drove them up to the curb of the hotel—the one Henry Perry was staying at. She couldn't explain it, but she felt like this was the true turning point of the whole case. She just hoped she was right.

Xander put the car in park, and Lily immediately opened the door. But Xander stopped her.

"Hey, Dawn, hold on," he said, and she looked in at him. He had a concerned look on his face. "Just be careful, all right? I'll call you once I interview my guy."

Lily smiled a little. "Thanks, Jackson. You stay safe too."

Lily slammed the door behind her, and seconds later, Xander peeled away. Lily looked up at the massive Florida hotel. The structure towered over Lily, its white walls standing tall and proud. Its windows were tinted and sparkling, and the glass seemed to stretch forever up into the morning sky. Large, ornate balconies decorated the front of the building, and a large fountain glistened in the middle of the courtyard. The doors were huge and inviting, like a grand gateway to an unknown world.

It was just the type of place the killer liked to hunt in. Lily had worked many cases in her career as an FBI agent, and she knew this feeling—when she was really onto something. She felt it now.

The killer… he could be here.

Lily took a deep breath and stepped forward, her feet crunching on the gravel beneath her shoes. She approached the hotel, feeling a strange mix of anticipation and dread as she did.

When Lily walked through the front doors, she was met with an elaborate lobby. The walls were draped in luxurious velvet curtains, and golden chandeliers hung from the ceiling. A large marble reception desk stood at one end of the lobby, attended by two uniformed staff members chatting quietly. On either side of them were matching couches with cream-colored cushions, inviting visitors to take their time and relax.

Lily took it all in for a moment and then walked up to the desk. The two staff members looked up at her expectantly, their eyes full of curiosity as they waited for her to speak. She held up her badge, and the girls' eyes widened.

"Good morning, ladies," Lily said. "I'm Agent Dawn with the FBI. I'm looking for a man who I think might be staying here. Can you help me with that?"

"Of course," the one girl, a redhead, said. "What's his name?"

"Henry Perry," Lily said. "He has heavy scarring on his face and body, so you might recognize him. Or maybe he was wearing winter clothing."

"Oh, there was someone here like that," the other girl, a brunette, said. "A guy wearing lots of layers, I thought it was super creepy and weird! We asked him what he was up to, as he was just kind of wandering around the lobby, and then he asked to check into a room."

Lily's heart raced. This could be it.

"I need to know his room number and be given the access card," Lily said.

The redhead nodded and quickly typed something into the computer. "Room 418," she said, handing Lily a keycard. "Be careful."

Lily thanked them both and hurried to the elevator. She swiped the keycard in the slot, and the doors opened with a loud ding. Inside, she pressed the number 4 button, her heart pounding with anticipation as she went up.

When the elevator doors opened, Lily stepped out and looked around. The hallways were brightly lit and carpeted with plush rugs. Door after door lined the hallway, each one numbered in gold lettering. She spotted number 418 and quickly made her way forward. She raised her hand to knock on the door, but no sound came out of her mouth.

Lily took a deep breath, trying to quell her nerves, and shook off the sense of dread that was slowly creeping up on her. With determination in her step she walked up to room 418 and knocked firmly three times. No one answered.

"Henry Perry?" Lily called out, knocking again. "This is the FBI. Open up, I need to talk to you. If you don't comply, I'm coming in."

Lily felt for the shape of her gun in its holster. It was there, safe. She could do this.

Lily stepped back and stood to the side of the doorway. She took a deep breath, steadied her nerves, put the keycard into the slot, and opened the door.

The room was empty. Lily stepped inside cautiously and looked around. There was no sign of Henry Perry anywhere, but there was a suitcase on the bed.

Lily walked over to the suitcase and opened it up. Inside, she found a stack of fashion magazines with various models wearing the latest clothing trends. She flipped through one of them—only to realize that the models on the pages inside had all been cut out. Lily flipped through more pages. Every fashion model, all cut out to leave a blank spot in the pages. What the hell?

Lily felt a chill run down her spine. Could this be evidence of something sinister? She quickly pocketed one of the magazines and glanced around the room again, making sure she hadn't missed anything important. Just then, she noticed a pile of clothes in the corner—winter clothes.

Lily's heart raced as she searched further around the room and found even more evidence of Henry's presence. She also noticed several more stacks of fashion magazines with strange designs cut out from them—some very intricate patterns that could only have been done with precision scissors or a sharp blade.

Clearly whatever Henry was up to involved modifying fashion magazines in some way—but why? Lily couldn't help but feel disturbed by all these clues pointing toward Henry Perry's obsession with mutilating fashion magazines. What did it mean? Did this all play into his psyche of hating the beautiful, perhaps in a vengeful way, since he was scarred from the fire he'd experienced as a child?

Maybe he was looking for some kind of closure, using the magazines as a way to cope with his own physical insecurities.

Lily couldn't help but wonder what Henry's motivations could be. Was he trying to make a statement against beauty? Could his past trauma have caused him to lash out at models of perfection, and was that why he had been so obsessed with cutting out the models from the magazines?

Or was it something darker? Did Henry have an even more sinister plan in mind, one that could potentially hurt innocent people? Lily had no way of knowing, but she knew she needed to find out. She had to get to the bottom of this mystery before Henry caused any more harm than he already had. This was all extremely sinister and pointed to something more evil. Lily was sure of it.

She took out her phone and called Xander, and he picked up immediately.

"Dawn, we have a problem."

"What is it?" Lily asked. She wanted to tell him what she'd found, but he talked first.

"The guy I'm after, Augustus—he's in a wheelchair, broke his leg pretty bad last week and that's why he's staying here, to avoid traveling. It just happened, so I didn't see it on his record."

"Jackson, it's okay—I don't think Augustus is the guy. I'm in Henry Perry's hotel room and there's some disturbing stuff in here. Mutilated fashion magazines. I think he might be hunting another victim right here, right now."

"Shit. I'm calling backup, and I'll be there as fast as I can. Oh—one more thing. Roger Pearson, the dead guy in the sauna, died of a heart attack. No foul play suspected."

"Good," Lily said. "At least we can close the book on that one." She turned to the door. "I'm gonna try to find Henry Perry right now. Please hurry."

Lily rushed out of the room, her mind racing with questions and fears. She had to find Henry Perry before it was too late. They'd already lost three people—they couldn't add another to the list.

Lily just hoped she wasn't too late. She'd worked so many cases, but none quite like this one. As she ran toward the elevator, she couldn't help the onslaught of memories—memories of her time in the FBI.

She remembered the first day she had arrived at the FBI field office, full of energy and enthusiasm. She had been immediately thrown into her first case—a homicide investigation—and was determined to make a name for herself as one of the best agents in the Bureau.

The hours were long, but Lily enjoyed every minute of it. She loved talking to witnesses and suspects, conducting interviews, analyzing evidence, and seeing justice served. It was fascinating work that never stopped challenging her.

The first case she cracked, the feeling of accomplishment when she finally put all the pieces together, the excitement of finding clues in the most unlikely places, and how it felt to be part of a team with a shared purpose—it had been an amazing experience, one that Lily would never forget.

Her days with the FBI had taught Lily so much; not just about criminal justice, but also about herself. She'd learned to trust her instincts and rely on her own judgment. She'd become more confident in her ability to handle difficult cases and take on tougher challenges.

Lily was determined to find Henry Perry and put an end to his reign of terror before anyone else was hurt—she owed it to those innocent victims who had already lost their lives. As she rode the elevator toward her destination, she couldn't help but feel a wave of pride for herself—she'd come so far from where she started as an FBI agent, and now here she was doing what she loved most—hunting down criminals and bringing them to justice.

And Henry Perry—he would be next on the long list of criminals taken down by Lily Dawn.

CHAPTER TWENTY TWO

Lily quickly made her way through the hotel, her footsteps echoing off the walls. She looked around frantically for any sign of Henry, but he seemed to have vanished into thin air. Instead, she was surrounded by tourists and normal people wandering around the hotel. Henry had to be here somewhere, but he could be anywhere—the sooner backup arrived with Xander, the better, but until then, Lily was on her own.

She stopped one of the guests and flashed her badge. "Have you seen a man in a winter coat anywhere?" she asked, her voice urgent.

The guest shook their head, their eyes wide with curiosity and confusion. "No, I haven't seen anyone like that here today," they replied. Lily thanked them before quickly continuing on her search. She had to find Henry before it was too late—every second counted now.

She rushed up to a staff member, who was making their way through the hall.

"Excuse me, have you seen a man in a winter coat?" Lily asked, once again flashing her badge. Wide-eyed, the employee shook their head.

Damn it! Lily didn't know where to go, so she just dashed through the hotel, looking for any signs of the man.

But despite her best efforts, she couldn't find anyone who had seen Henry. No one had even seen him enter the hotel in the first place. He was like a ghost—here one second and gone the next.

Lily stopped in her tracks, feeling defeated. She had failed to find Henry before he could cause any more harm, and now it was too late. She'd been so close, but still hadn't been able to catch him in time…

No! She couldn't give up. Lily took a deep breath and squared her shoulders. She had come this far, and she was not going to give up now. She was determined to make a name for herself as one of the best agents in the Bureau, and if that meant finding Henry Perry, then so be it.

She pushed forward, her determination fueling her every step. She would not back down until she found Henry and put an end to his reign of terror once and for all. Lily had made up her mind—nothing was going to stand in her way. After all, that's what the best agents do—never give up until justice is served.

Lily had learned that most of all from her mentor, Special Agent Frank Foster. His mentorship still followed her in everything she did, even if he had retired.

She remembered how he had always pushed her to take on more difficult cases and take on tougher challenges. He had encouraged her to do the best she could, no matter the circumstances, and had given her the courage to make decisions that were right for her and for the case.

Whenever she felt overwhelmed or out of her depth, Foster was there to give her a pep talk and remind her why she joined the FBI in the first place. He'd always believed in her and been proud of what she was doing, and through all the difficult cases they faced together, Lily knew Foster had always been by her side, cheering her on, even with his gruff exterior.

He had been the one who taught her to never give up and that no case was too difficult to handle. He had instilled in her a sense of courage and faith that she could tackle any challenge, no matter how hard it seemed.

His words echoed in Lily's mind as she continued down the corridor, giving her the strength she needed to keep going. She remembered his lessons about trusting herself and being brave when faced with danger.

Lily found herself in a common area, and up ahead, she spotted a bulletin board. On it were several advertisements, and Lily saw one showed several women in bikinis. It was a bikini contest being hosted on a stage out the back of the hotel—the exact type of place someone with the mentality of the killer might go to hunt for victims. If he was angered by beauty and the like, then this was it—this was the place he was going.

Without another thought, Lily ran outside. The sun was scorching and the heat smacked her in the face, but she didn't care. She had to find Henry before it was too late, no matter what it took.

Lily made her way around the back of the hotel, following the signs for the bikini contest. As she got closer, she could see a large stage erected with several women standing on it in their beachwear, posing for spectators and judges alike. There were people everywhere—some admiring the contestants, some taking pictures or videos—but none of them looked like Henry.

Lily scanned every face as she moved closer to the stage, desperate to find him somewhere in the crowd. But she didn't see him.

There was music blasting, and the event was full of people. It was so busy, and Lily could feel her heart racing as she searched the faces of the guests. It seemed like everyone was there to watch the bikini contest and have a good time, but Lily knew that just beneath the surface lay danger. She had to be vigilant if she had any chance of finding Henry.

Vendors had set up shops, and others were selling refreshments. People were laughing and chatting, snacking on traditional beachside snacks like hotdogs and nachos. It was a lively atmosphere, but Lily couldn't help but feel a sense of dread as she looked around for Henry.

She stopped a man, who looked at her in confusion.

"Excuse me, have you seen a man in a winter coat? I'm looking for a man in a winter coat!"

The guy just shrugged. Lily grunted in frustration—she didn't have time for this—and moved on to the next person, a young woman watching the stage.

"Have you seen a man in a winter coat?" Lily asked.

The woman shook her head, and Lily felt her heart sink—she was running out of options. She continued along the crowd, asking anyone she could find if they had seen Henry, but all she received were blank stares or shrugs. Until finally, she stopped one last person—a girl in her mid-twenties.

"Have you seen a man in a winter coat?" she asked desperately. But at this point, it was starting to feel futile.

But the girl, wide-eyed, said, "Um… yeah, actually, I did."

Lily almost thought she hadn't heard her right. All this asking around, and finally, a potential answer.

"You did?!" Lily's heart raced. "Where? Please, this is very important!"

The girl pointed behind them, to a large building separate from the rest of the hotel. If Lily had to guess, that was the maintenance shed, and probably held things like lawn mowers and equipment used to keep the hotel in top shape.

Without wasting another second, Lily beelined it to the maintenance building. Her heart was pounding as she approached the door, and she tried desperately to stay calm. If Henry was in there, then this could be her last chance to catch him before he could do any more harm.

As she got closer, she could see that the door was closed. Her heart pounded in her chest as she crept closer, then tried the door, but it was locked. She peered inside a window. It was dark, but there was enough light streaming in from outside for her to make out the shapes of the equipment inside.

But no sign of Henry.

Lily's heart sank. Had she been wrong? She had been so certain he would be here, but it seemed like her hunch had been wrong. She stepped away from the building, her mind spinning with despair and confusion. Where the hell was backup? She needed more bodies to cover this much ground.

Just as Lily was about to go search somewhere else, she heard it:

A scream. From inside the maintenance building.

Lily's resolve burst into life. She looked inside the maintenance building again, and that was when she saw it—a woman, running through the building, dodging past a row of lawn mowers. Lily couldn't see who she was running from—but she had a pretty damn good idea.

Henry Perry. It had to be him. He was here, and he was hunting his next kill—but Lily wasn't too late. She just needed to get in that building.

She ran back to the door and tried the knob again, but it was still locked. She kicked it hard, but it didn't budge. She tried to pry the door open with her fingers, but that didn't work either. Finally, she took a step back and rammed her shoulder into the door. The wood creaked and splintered from the force of her impact—but it refused to open.

Desperate, Lily looked around for something she could use as a weapon or tool—and then spotted a rock nearby on the ground. She picked up the rock and slammed it against the padlock securing the door shut—but even after several blows, all she had managed to do was chip away at its surface. She needed something bigger, something more powerful if she wanted to get inside in time and save that woman's life.

Lily felt her heart race as she searched for something else to help her break down the door—but there was nothing else in sight. Each second seemed like an eternity as Lily waited desperately for help to arrive while Henry chased his victim within feet of her reach.

Damn it! She didn't have time for this. Instead, Lily grabbed the rock and made a quick decision. She turned around, ran a few steps away from the door and then launched the rock at the large window beside it.

The window shattered with a loud crash, and shards of glass flew everywhere.

Lily didn't hesitate—she rushed through the broken window and into the maintenance building to save another life.

Lily landed inside. The room was still and dimly lit, illuminated only by the faint light coming in from the broken window. The floor was littered with pieces of shattered glass, and the air was heavy with a stifling silence. There was no sign of the predator or his victim—just an all-encompassing hush that seemed to swallow up anything that moved. A stale musty smell hung in the air, a combination of dust and mold and old machinery. The scent of desperation lingered, as if the killer had left a scent of his malice in his wake.

Lily wasted no time. She ran through the hallway, searching for Henry or his victim, but all she found was darkness and emptiness. She checked every corner of the building, every nook and cranny—but her search yielded nothing. The killer had disappeared without a trace. But he had to be here.

Lily began to search the building, her eyes darting back and forth as she carefully inspected every corner of the room. She wanted to make sure that Henry wasn't hiding in some dark nook, waiting for his next chance at a victim. Yet despite her thorough investigation, Lily couldn't find any trace of him.

She had searched every room in the building already—but there was still one place left to look: the basement. Lily took a deep breath before she opened the door and peered down into the darkness below, her heart pounding against her chest like a drumbeat. The staircase leading down seemed endless, stretching down into an abyss of shadows and secrets. But after taking one hesitant step forward, Lily forced herself onward, determined to find Henry and bring him to justice.

She descended deeper into the darkness, searching through forgotten corners and abandoned tools until she reached the bottom of the stairs—and came face-to-face with an empty space that felt like a tomb. Nothing stirred here except for cobwebs dangling from rafters above—Henry Perry was nowhere to be found.

But then, just as Lily was about to leave, she heard a noise. A shuffling up ahead.

Someone was here.

Before Lily could go forward, she felt something hard and metal whack the back of her head.

Then, darkness.

CHAPTER TWENTY THREE

"All right, people, listen up!" Xander said to the police officers outside of the hotel. They'd all arrived around the same time, and Xander needed them to know exactly what they were here for. Lily was in there somewhere, looking for the killer—and Xander needed to be there for her.

It could be life or death for a lot of people—Lily included, and that scared him more than anything. He couldn't lose his partner, not like this, and not on his watch.

He focused on the officers. "The man you're looking for is Henry Perry, he's a thirty-something burn victim with heavy scarring and might be dressed in winter clothing. You need to look through every inch of this place—this guy is dangerous. He's a goddamn serial killer, so you need to be extremely cautious and vigilant. You got that?"

The officers nodded, and Xander breathed a sigh of relief. It seemed like he had a good team on his hands. They were ready to go in—and so was he.

They all moved forward, cautiously entering the building. Xander's heart was pounding as he headed into the hotel, his stomach aching with fear and anticipation. He had to find Lily—had to make sure she was safe.

He broke off from the cops and began his own search, starting with the pool area out back—he'd heard a lot of commotion, loud music and cheering, so maybe there was some sort of event going on.

Xander walked the perimeter of the pool area, his eyes darting around as he searched for any sign of Henry. He kept his ears open too—the faint sound of singing in the distance could be heard, but otherwise there was nothing out of the ordinary. He looked around the pool area carefully, inspecting every corner and every crevice, but he found nothing but hotel guests giving him strange looks. He couldn't be bothered with any of them, but he had to ask:

"Hey, you three," he said to a group of people tanning. They looked at him, confused. "You see a blonde woman dressed professionally coming through here? Or a guy in a winter coat?"

"We saw some lady looking for a guy in a winter coat," one guy said. "She was asking everyone."

"Where'd she go?" Xander asked, his heart racing.

"I think I saw her go through to the back," a girl said. "They're having a bikini contest out there."

"A bikini contest?" Xander said, eyebrows raised.

"Yeah, it's a tradition around here," one of them said.

He didn't have time to think about it now. He thanked the group and ran off toward the back of the hotel, adrenaline coursing through his body.

When he arrived at the back of the hotel, he saw what they had been talking about. There was a makeshift stage with several women wearing bright bikinis and high heels—they were competing for some kind of prize or trophy. The crowd cheered as each woman strutted her stuff, while a team of judges watched intently from their seats on stage. The women onstage were dancing and performing for the crowd. Xander's eyes scanned the audience, looking for Lily. There were so many faces.

He walked through the throngs of people, his eyes darting from face to face, searching for her. He saw couples and families and groups of friends—but no Lily. He kept going, pushing himself further and further into the crowd, looking for any sign of her. He tried to listen out too—maybe he'd hear her voice. But all he could hear was the music and the cheering of the crowd.

He felt a sinking feeling in his stomach as he realized that she wasn't here. He had lost her in the chaos—and it was his job to find her again. He made his way through the crowd, keeping an eye out for Lily or Henry Perry as he went. No luck.

He broke off from the crowd—there was too much chaos, too much chatter. The sun beamed down on him, making him sweat. Pulling his phone out of his pocket, he tried to call Lily again, but it just kept ringing with no answer.

He felt a wave of panic wash over him. He had to find her—she was in danger, and he didn't know where she was.

"Damn it, Dawn, where are you?"

If she were just searching around, she'd answer his call. She always did. No, Xander felt it—something was wrong.

It was strange to him how much he cared, in all honesty. Of course he valued human life—why else would he have become an FBI agent? But with Lily, it was just… different. He'd had partners before, but he was worried about her in a way he didn't worry about them.

He had never realized just how much Lily meant to him until this moment. He could feel it in his bones, a deep-seated need to protect her and keep her safe. He knew she could take care of herself—she was a damn strong woman—but that was why he was so drawn to her. She didn't need him, not at all, and maybe that was why he felt like he needed her.

It was bad for business, he realized. Was he developing some sort of romantic inkling for her? Sure, she'd always been gorgeous in his eyes, but Xander's love life was complicated; he was still in contact with his ex. But he'd been feeling something for Lily more and more as they worked together.

Coming from a rough background like he did—drunk parents and siblings, a Texas trailer park upbringing—he'd never been good at settling down, except with the FBI. But the FBI wasn't enough. He wanted a deeper connection—one he couldn't find with his job. He hated sounding like a suck, but that was what he'd been trying to forge with his ex, and that situation was just a nightmare.

Xander had never had much stability, and he got the sense Lily was the same way, what with her missing sister and her parents not talking to her and all. In a lot of ways, they were alike.

He shook his head and took a deep breath, trying to clear it of any thoughts that weren't related to finding her. He had to stay focused if he was going to locate her in time. He began walking again, determined not to let anything stand in his way of helping Lily Dawn. He just needed to find Lily and make sure she was safe.

He began to make his way around the building, looking for any sign of her.

Xander's gaze shifted from the stage to the maintenance building, just a few yards away from where he was standing. The door was shut and barred, but one of the windows on the second floor had been broken—the glass shattered and lying on the ground outside.

He paused. Shit—maybe she was in there. Was this an exit route for Lily? Xander quickly ran toward it, hoping that Lily hadn't gotten herself into something she couldn't get out of. On a whim, he avoided the glass and jumped into the maintenance building. It was dark and quiet inside, and the air was thick with the smell of oil and grass. Xander had his eyes peeled for any sign of movement, but there was nothing. It felt like a ghost town. But then something made him stop in his tracks—the smell of desperation lingered in the air, like a warning sign to stay away.

Xander could feel it deep in his gut—something was wrong here.

He could feel the hair on the back of his neck stand up and a chill run down his spine. His mind was racing, a million thoughts running through his head all at once. What if Lily was in danger? What if she had been taken hostage? Despite all of the fear and anxiety coursing through him, Xander pressed on, determined to find her no matter what. He knew that he had to act fast and be brave—it was the only way he'd be able to help her.

He moved through the building slowly, peering into each room carefully in case someone or something was lurking inside. He kept walking until he came across a door that was slightly ajar. As he gently pushed it open, a faint light shone from inside, illuminating an empty room with nothing but old furniture scattered around it.

Xander stepped inside, surveying the area for signs of life or clues as to where Lily might have gone. No luck.

He continued searching, finding nothing but another empty room. He stepped out of the building and started to walk around the area, looking for any clue that could lead him to Lily. He searched high and low, but there was no sign of her.

Where the hell are you, Dawn?

On a fragile hope, Xander took his phone out again and called her. It rang and rang, but she didn't pick up. But he heard something, somewhere in the building…

Xander froze and held his breath. It was the faint vibration of Lily's phone, coming from somewhere inside the building. Xander ran toward the sound, his heart pounding in his chest. He followed the noise until he came to set of stairs leading down into a basement cellar area. His eyes widened as he realized what it was—it was Lily's phone, lying on the ground and still vibrating from his incoming call.

Xander's heart sank to his stomach.

Lily was in danger.

CHAPTER TWENTY FOUR

Lily's eyes fluttered open. The back of her head throbbed, and on instinct, she reached back, only to feel warm blood matting the back of her hair. She was lying on cold concrete… what happened?

As Lily's eyes adjusted, she realized she was in a dimly lit room—and she wasn't alone. A woman—the girl she'd seen earlier—was tied up in the corner of the room, and there was a man pacing violently across the room, wearing a massive winter jacket and a hat, with a scarf covering his face.

"No… no… this ruins everything! One, I could get away with, but two? I can't do this… I'm caught… I have to kill them both… but then where can I stage them?"

On wobbly legs, Lily managed to stand, reaching for her gun—but it was gone. As soon as he realized she was up, the man turned to her with wild eyes. She couldn't see most of his face, but beneath his hat, she made out the skin around his eyes—it was covered in scarring. Burn scars.

Henry Perry.

The back of Lily's head throbbed. Beside Henry, on the ground, was a shovel. He must have hit Lily over the head with it. The girl across the room looked at Lily with wide, teary eyes, and with the sock stuffed in her mouth, she could only make noises.

"Stay right there," Henry said to Lily. "Don't move. I'm still figuring out what to do with you. But I'm all out of zip ties… oh, I should just shoot you with your own gun… but that would be such a waste!"

Lily swallowed hard and tried to stay calm. "Henry," she said, trying to keep her voice steady. "Please don't do anything hasty. You don't want this. I can help you, if you just talk to me."

She kept her hands up in the air as she slowly stepped toward him. The girl across the room was shaking now, tears streaming down her face as she silently pleaded for help with her eyes.

"Stay back!" Henry yelled, taking a step back and covering his face with his arm again as if he were hiding from something—or someone—invisible. He shook his head in disbelief and began ranting wildly about how life had been unfair to him and that he'd been wronged by society for far too long.

Lily continued walking slowly toward him, never breaking eye contact or dropping her gaze from his face.

"Henry," she said, her voice shaking. "Let's talk this out. I know you didn't mean to do any of this… it was an accident."

Henry looked at Lily with rage in his eyes, and he pulled the gun out of his pocket, pointing it right at her. Lily would have flinched, but judging by the way he was holding it, he didn't know how to use it. Still, a gun was a dangerous thing in anyone's hands, and she had to proceed with caution.

"Shut up! Don't try to talk me out of this! I have to do what I have to do!"

Lily swallowed hard and tried again.

"No, Henry," she said calmly. "You don't have to do anything—you can just let us go free. No one will ever know you were here."

"I know what you are," he said. "You're the FBI. You're going to try to lock me away. I won't survive in prison. I barely survived the foster care system. They mocked me endlessly… they'll eat me alive in prison!"

Lily took a deep breath and held her hands out in front of her. "Henry, I'm not here to lock you away," she said softly. "I'm here to help you. All I want is for us to get out of this safely—all three of us. Can you let us go?"

Henry paused and looked at Lily, then at the girl across the room, and finally back at Lily. His grip on the gun loosened ever so slightly, and he lowered it just a bit, though his eyes still flashed with fear.

"Please," Lily implored him gently. "Let us go free—you don't have to do anything else."

"No," he said, malice in his eyes. "No! You're just like the rest of them, you stereotypical bitch! You think you can just make me do anything you say because you're beautiful? Well, beauty is nothing! It's worth nothing! You're just a waste of life, trying to get through everything with your looks!"

"That's not true at all, Henry," Lily said. "I'm an FBI agent, Henry. My looks have nothing to do with it."

"Bullshit! You only got hired because of your beauty! If you looked like me, no one would let you do anything!"

Lily took a deep breath and stepped closer to him. She could feel the tension radiating off of him, and she knew that if she acted too quickly he would panic.

"Henry," she said in a soft, soothing voice. "You're wrong about that. My skills got me this job—not my looks. You're just as smart and capable as I am, if not more so. I'm here to help you, not hurt you. You don't have to do anything hasty. We can talk this out."

It seemed to be working.

She paused for a moment, letting her words sink in before continuing. "You don't have to do anything you don't want to do," she said softly. "You don't have to let anger control your life any longer—you can choose a different path if you just take the time to think about it rationally."

Henry's grip on the gun loosened further, his eyes losing some of their rage as he digested Lily's words. She took another step forward and placed her hand gently on his shoulder, her eyes never leaving his face as she smiled encouragingly at him.

"It's okay," she said softly. "We all make mistakes—it doesn't define who we are or what we can become in the future." She paused again and squeezed his shoulder reassuringly before continuing.

"Take a deep breath, Henry," she said calmly. "Let go of your fear and anger for just a second—find something else inside of yourself that will help guide you through this."

For a moment, Lily almost felt like she was truly getting to him. She was close to him, and he wasn't reacting. Just a couple more steps, and she could disarm him and take control of the gun.

But then, it all changed. Henry suddenly snapped and his grip on the gun tightened again. He shoved Lily away from him and pointed the gun directly at her face. His eyes were wide with rage, and he screamed at her in a voice full of hate.

"This is all your fault," he yelled as he advanced toward her. "You think you can just waltz in here and change everything? You think you can just control me like I'm some puppet? Well guess what, I'm not! I won't let anyone control me ever again!"

Lily stepped back slowly, fear gripping her heart as she watched Henry come closer and closer to her. She knew that if he reached her there was no chance of getting out alive—he'd probably shoot them both without a second thought. As she continued moving backwards, trying desperately to find an escape route, she could feel the girl behind her cowering in fear as well.

Suddenly, Henry lunged forward with a roar of fury and grabbed hold of Lily's arm, yanking her close to him as he raised the gun threateningly above his head. But that gave Lily the perfect opening. She shot her arm up and punched him in the right spot on his forearm that made him instantly drop the gun. Before Lily could grab the gun, Henry lunged at her and tackled her to the ground, sending a fist flying toward her face. His heavy winter clothes made him feel even bulkier, and Lily defensively covered her face with her forearms.

With all her strength, she pushed him off of her and scrambled away from him, quickly grabbing the gun and pointing it back at him. Henry froze in place, his eyes widening in shock as he stared down the barrel of the gun. Lily had taken control of the situation and was now standing tall and confident with a gun pointed at him.

"Don't move," she said firmly. "I don't want to hurt you, but I will if I have to."

Henry stared at her for a moment and then backed away slowly, his eyes never leaving hers. He knew that she meant business and he didn't want to make things worse for himself by trying something foolish.

Despite her fear, Lily held her ground firmly, her heart pounding as she prepared herself for whatever would happen next. She could feel the girl behind her trembling as they watched Henry carefully take another step back toward the door.

At that same moment, someone burst inside behind him. Henry yelled out and went to run—but it was Xander's body blocking the doorframe now.

Lily let out a massive breath of relief. Xander was here, and the moment he saw Lily had taken control of the situation, he grabbed Henry and twisted his arms behind his back, slapping cuffs on him.

"Jackson, you came!" Lily said, and he shot her a quick smile as Henry writhed beneath the cuffs.

"Sorry I was late, Lils."

Without wasting another second, Lily dove toward the girl who had been tied up and freed her, pulling the gag from her mouth.

"Thank you," the girl said, her voice quivering as she hugged Lily tightly. "You saved me. You saved us both."

Lily smiled warmly and nodded, squeezing the girl's shoulder gently in reassurance. She was relieved that everything had worked out okay, but also overwhelmed by all the emotions of the situation.

"It's alright," Lily whispered softly to the victim. "You're safe now."

The girl thanked Lily through tear-filled eyes for saving her life, and expressed her immense gratitude for coming when she did and having enough courage to take control of such a dangerous situation. She knew that if it wasn't for Lily, she could have been hurt or worse—and only because of her bravery was she still safe and sound.

Lily felt a wave of pride wash over her knowing that she had made a difference by using her skills to protect another person from harm—something she hadn't been able to do for herself in years. She gave the victim one last hug before turning away with Xander at her side, glad to know that justice would be served.

Henry Perry was a twisted man. But he'd never hurt anyone else again.

CHAPTER TWENTY FIVE

"Well, you two did it again," Chief Aboye said, sitting across from Lily and Xander at her office at the FBI HQ in Miami. Lily felt proud as she faced the chief, happy she was here to deliver good news about a job well done—happy they'd been able to save the final victim and put an end to Henry's short reign of terror.

"Thank you, Chief," Lily said. "We had a couple of low points, but I'm glad we saved the girl."

"I'm sure she's grateful too," Chief Aboye said with a light chuckle, a smile on her dark face. "I just knew you two'd make a great team."

Beside Lily, Xander shot Lily a smile that she caught in her peripheral vision.

"You did a fantastic job," the chief said, her voice filled with admiration. "Not everyone can take on such a dangerous situation without fear or hesitation—but you two did it with courage and determination. I'm very proud of you two."

Chief Aboye's words struck a chord within Lily, and she felt her chest swell with pride. She'd gone through so much to get here—years of struggles, obstacles, and pain—and now she was finally making a difference.

She looked at Xander and saw the same look in his eye as he glanced at her from the side—a feeling of accomplishment for doing something good for someone else. It wasn't just about getting justice for the victims anymore—it was about making sure no one ever had to go through what they went through again.

"You've both come so far," Chief Aboye continued, her eyes twinkling with admiration. "You have sharp minds and brave hearts; it's no wonder that you were able to catch Henry Perry so quickly."

The chief paused to take a sip of her coffee before leaning forward in her chair and fixing both Lily and Xander with an intense gaze. The chief reached out her hand and shook Lily's, then Xander's—a gesture of respect that warmed Lily's heart. She knew that this was a big moment for both of them, and she was grateful for the opportunity.

"Thank you kindly, Chief," Xander said with a nod of his head.

"Yes, thank you so much," Lily added in agreement.

"The pleasure is mine," said the chief. "Lily, I know you left an important personal matter to come in, and I'm truly grateful for that. I'd like to give you both a full week off—no exceptions."

Lily smiled, relief flowing through her. As much as she valued working here, she also needed to get back to Aruba and see her parents before it was too late.

"Thank you, Chief," Lily said.

"Of course. When you come back, I'm sure I'll have a new assignment waiting for you, so enjoy the time off. You're both dismissed."

Lily and Xander stood up, both feeling a sense of accomplishment. They had done the right thing, and justice would be served. As they made their way out of the chief's office, Lily felt a hand on her shoulder—Xander's hand. She turned to look at him, and he smiled back at her, his eyes twinkling with admiration.

"We did it," he said softly.

Lily smiled in agreement as they stepped out into the hallway together. It was late in the evening now, and the corridor was mostly empty except for a few security guards patrolling the area. The lights were dimmed, giving everything an almost dreamy quality.

"Hey, Dawn," Xander said, hooking his hand to the back of his neck. Lily shot him an inquisitive look, and for a moment, he almost looked like a school boy. "Mind having a word with me in my office?"

Lily raised her eyebrows in surprise but nodded in agreement. She followed Xander down the hallway, her heart pounding with anticipation. She wasn't sure, but something seemed different about Xander. They went into his office, and Lily was met with the familiar smell of patchouli. Xander closed the door, securing them in the room, alone together. Lily wandered over toward Xander's desk and sat on the edge of it, facing him as he continued to rub the back of his neck.

"What's going on?" Lily asked.

"I just wanted to say, personally, that I'm glad I was partnered up with you. I know I can be a pain the ass, but you keep me in line."

Lily's heart warmed. What had him being so nice? "Well, thank you, Jackson," she managed. "I'm glad I'm with you too."

Xander smiled and took a step closer to her, so close that she could feel the warmth radiating off of him. She felt her cheeks flush as he looked into her eyes.

"You know what? I think we should celebrate," Xander said finally. "Grab a drink with me sometime?"

Lily was taken aback by his sudden invitation. She had no idea what to say; all she could do was stare at him in shock. Maybe she was imagining it, but it almost seemed like he was asking her on a date.

Xander was a good-looking guy, she couldn't deny that. He had blond hair and green eyes with a tanned complexion, and he was tall and lean, and always dressed sharp. But he was her partner…

Lily wasn't quite sure what to say. She could feel the butterflies in her stomach starting to flutter again, and she suddenly felt very aware of how close they were standing.

"You don't gotta answer now," Xander said. "I know you need to hurry back to Aruba and see your folks. But when you're back, before we start work again, maybe we could try to get to know each other as, you know, people. Not just FBI agents."

Lily smiled, feeling her heart swell with warmth. She realized that she wanted to get to know Xander better, too. Maybe it wasn't romantic—maybe it didn't need to be. All Lily knew was that she liked this feeling, like he was trying to get to know her.

"Yes," Lily finally said. "When I'm back, let's go for a drink."

He smiled, dimples and all. "Looking forward to it, Agent Dawn."

CHAPTER TWENTY SIX

Lily hurried up to her parents' door in Aruba, surrounded by the familiar smell of the nighttime streets. The stars splashed in the sky above; Lily had taken a late plane in, and now she was back again, as though she hadn't even left. The air was filled with a mix of salty ocean air and fragrant tropical flora. It was a comforting smell that reminded Lily of home; in many ways, it still felt so surreal to actually be here.

But she also knew her parents might not be so thrilled she came and left so quickly. Especially her mother. They already had such a strained relationship.

Ever since Kara disappeared, Lily's mom had been less forgiving than her father. She was never really mean, but she had been so cold and so distant, and so different from the woman Lily knew growing up.

Before Kara's disappearance, Lily and her mom had been so close. They used to bake together, walk through the botanical garden, and go on trips around Aruba. Her mother was always so kind and understanding. She would listen to all of Lily's stories without judgment, and help her with anything she needed.

Swallowing her nerves, Lily knocked on the door. Within moments, her father answered, wearing pajamas.

"Lily!" he exclaimed. "You actually came back!"

"I told you I would, Dad," Lily pointed out, trying to mask how guilty she really felt.

He stepped aside to let her in. "Your mother's still up, watching TV in the living room. She's been waiting for you."

Lily tried to ignore the sinking feeling that was forming in her stomach as she followed her father inside the house. She knew it wasn't going to be an easy conversation, but she was determined to make it work.

She entered the living room and found her mother sitting on the couch, a blanket draped around her shoulders as she watched an old movie on television. Lily smiled tentatively and walked over to join her.

"Hi, Mom," she said softly.

Her mother looked up from the TV and gave Lily a long look before finally speaking. "You're back," she said simply.

Lily took a deep breath and nodded, hoping her mother could tell how much effort this had taken for her. "Yes," Lily replied quietly, taking a seat beside her mother on the couch. "I'm sorry I left like that. Work called, and it was, well… I couldn't miss it."

"Did it go okay?" her mother asked hesitantly.

Lily smiled. "We put a really bad man behind bars."

In many ways, Lily felt bad for Henry Perry. She knew his disfigurement was a great source of anxiety for him, and his life hadn't been easy. Regardless, that never gave him the right to kill, so behind bars was where he belonged. Due to his concerns, though, Lily requested that he be given his own cell, and he was put in a ward of the prison where they mainly kept disabled prisoners. It was the best chance Lily could give Henry at avoiding the ridicule that had plagued him for most of his life. If he was with other people who were different, maybe they would be less hard on him. It was all beyond Lily's control now; unfortunately, the only thing that could have saved Henry was if he'd never killed at all.

But he had. Those lives would never be given back, so Henry had to give his in return. Still, Lily hoped his suffering could be minimized.

This was all too much to dump on her parents, of course—she hadn't come to see them to tell them about the horrors of being in the FBI, the hard choices that had to be made for the greater good.

"It's really nice to see you, Mom," Lily said.

"It's nice to see you too," her mom managed. "It's… a bit strange for me still. I mean, it has been ten years. But I'm glad to see you're well."

Lily nodded, feeling a sense of warmth from her mother's words. "Me too," she said softly.

The two of them sat in silence for a few moments as Lily watched the flickering light play across her mother's face. She had aged gracefully, and though they hadn't seen each other in so long, it felt like no time had passed at all.

Her mother sighed and looked up at the stars visible through the window. "This is where I used to bring you when you were a little girl," she said fondly. "We'd sit here for hours and watch the stars, talking about our dreams."

Lily chuckled softly, a wave of nostalgia washing over her as memories of those nights came flooding back. She couldn't believe how quickly time had passed. It felt like only yesterday they'd been sitting here on these very same couches, discussing life and love and all manner of things that seemed so important then but seemed almost trivial now in the grand scheme of things.

"It still feels like yesterday," Lily said wistfully.

Her mother laughed softly and nodded in agreement. "It does," she murmured before turning to face Lily directly once more. "And look at you now—you're all grown up, living your own life! Doing big things!" Her voice shook slightly as she spoke, as though holding back tears of pride or perhaps sorrow that her little girl had grown so quickly into a woman who could take on even the most sinister serial killers.

But a silence fell upon them and Lily's gut twisted.

"I just… wish your sister were here too," her mother said.

"Me too, Mom," Lily told her. And she meant it.

Lily recalled the other day when she was here, the strange occult books she'd found in Kara's room—it was all too weird to tell her parents about now. She wondered if they had seen the books before, but she doubted it. She wanted to learn more before she brought it up.

"Anyway, I'm just gonna go change into some pj's," Lily said, standing. "I'll be back down in a few."

"Of course, dear," her mom said.

Lily gave her mother a smile before making her way upstairs. As she reached Kara's bedroom, she felt a chill run up her spine—it was like the room still held the same energy and aura it had when Kara was alive. Lily stepped inside and ran her fingers along the posters on the wall and looked at the photos of Kara with friends that hung above her desk. The room still held a scent of familiarity, yet it was tinged with a hint of something foreign.

She went to the corner and pulled up the floorboard, uncovering the collection of books beneath it. She knelt down and examined them one by one. Before Kara disappeared, Lily had no memory of her ever being into alchemy or witchcraft or occult things, and yet here was all of the evidence. What could it mean?

Lily wondered why Kara had all these books, what she was trying to find out. She remembered her sister's curiosity and passion for learning, but this seemed like something more—like she was searching for something specific. Lily felt a wave of sadness wash over her; she knew that if only Kara were here, she could have asked her all the questions that now seemed so unanswered.

Lily was filled with a strange mixture of curiosity and concern as she flipped through the pages. She wondered what Kara had been searching for in these books, why she had chosen to keep this hidden from her family. Lily ran her fingers over the cover of one book, tracing the symbols on it with her eyes closed. What answers could these books provide? Was there some sort of power they held that Kara had sought after? These things weren't real—Lily knew that—but she also knew how many people believed in them. She wouldn't have expected her sister to be one of them.

As Lily sat there, she wondered who might know more. Her parents? Maybe, but no… Kara had friends, too. Best friends, in fact. She was in a tightknit group with three other girls, her three best friends, Ana, Vivian, and Astrid. Lily had talked to the girls before, but they all claimed they never heard from or saw Kara the night she disappeared.

But could they know something about these books?

Those four girls told each other everything, Lily knew that. Lily had never quite had friendships like that, but she knew Kara, Ana, Astrid, and Vivian were inseparable. They even called themselves KAAV.

Lily had a feeling that the answers to her questions about Kara's books were somehow connected to her friends. Maybe if she could find a way to talk to them, she'd have more of an understanding of what was going on.

Lily was filled with a spark of hope and determination as she put the books back and replaced the floorboard. She went downstairs, her heart pounding in her chest, determined to find out the truth about Kara's disappearance.

"Mom, Dad," Lily said breathlessly, "do you know if Kara's friends still live in Aruba?"

Her parents were both on the couch now, and they looked up.

"What friends?" her dad asked.

"You know, Ana, Astrid, and Vivian?" Lily asked.

"Oh, of course they do," her mom replied, but then her face went grim. "But honey," she continued, "I'm afraid that Ana passed away seven years ago."

Lily's heart sank. "What? Ana died?"

Lily felt a lump in her throat as her mom told her the news. She couldn't believe it. She remembered Ana being such a vibrant, beautiful person. She was always so full of life and joy when they were all together, always making everyone laugh. How could she be gone?

"What happened to her?" Lily asked.

"I don't know much," her mom said. "I… avoided looking into it, to be honest with you. It reminded me too much of Kara. It was too tragic to face."

Lily's pulse raced. If she could find at least one of the three girls, she could find out more about this apparent secret Kara had been keeping—and find out what happened to Ana.

She knew she had a lead, and if she pursued it, maybe she could finally get some answers about Kara's disappearance.

EPILOGUE

The next morning, Lily sat in the café surrounded by pastel-hued walls, adorned with potted plants and ivy. Sunlight washed through the airy windows. The café was filled with the scent of fresh-brewed coffee, buttery croissants, and creamy scrambled eggs. It was a mélange of sweet and savory aromas. Lily sipped her coffee and tasted a hint of caramel mixed with smooth roasted hazelnut. But as nice as it all was, Lily hadn't come here to enjoy herself.

She was waiting for Kara's friends to show up. Well… her remaining two friends.

How had Lily never been told of Ana's death? If Ana died seven years ago, then that would mean she passed three years after Kara's disappearance. What if there was a connection? It felt grossly negligent that Lily hadn't been made aware of this until now.

The clinking of porcelain against porcelain, silverware against plates, and low whispers between friends in the café echoed around her. Outside, gulls called to one another in the ocean breeze, the sound like a whisper in her ear. She'd been waiting for so long now and was starting to worry they wouldn't show up.

Lily had looked up what had happened to Ana. It turned out she'd died in an apparent drowning accident. That was how the police had theorized Kara had died too, although Kara's body was never found—so it couldn't be completely confirmed Kara was dead at all.

Just then, Lily heard a familiar voice coming from the cafe entrance. "Astrid! Vivian!" she called out, standing up quickly. Sure enough, it was Kara's friends. They both looked different than when Lily had last seen them seven years ago—older, more mature, their features slightly softened with time. Astrid was tanned with long, black hair while Vivian had lighter skin and dark brown hair. The girls awkwardly walked up to Lily's table.

"Lily… wow," Astrid said. "It's been so long. You look so…well, you look the same."

"She's somehow even hotter," Vivian pointed out. She'd always been the snarky one. "Seriously, Lily, we always thought you were the prettiest girl on the island. Kara always felt like she was in your shadow in that sense."

"What? I didn't know that," Lily said, feeling uncomfortable with the revelation. She hoped it was just gossip and not actually true. Kara had been beautiful; while Lily her their mom's blonde hair and blue eyes, Kara had their father's darker features. They both shared their father's darker complexion, though.

Astrid and Vivian sat across from Lily, fidgeting anxiously.

"Thanks for coming," Lily said.

"We wouldn't miss it," Astrid said. "We were really surprised to hear from you. It's been years."

Lily nodded solemnly. "I heard about Ana… my mother told me last night."

"You only just heard about that?" Vivian asked.

"Unfortunately," Lily commented. "I wish I'd known sooner. Do you know what happened to her?"

"She drowned, I guess," Astrid said. "We barely know anything either… she just like, disappeared one night, then I guess she washed up on shore."

"She disappeared first?" Lily asked.

The girls nodded. "It was strange," Vivian said. "We were all hanging out at the beach and we got distracted by something—we can't even remember what it was now—but when we looked back, Ana was gone."

"We searched for her until late into the night," Astrid continued. "But no one ever found her… not until two weeks later, when they found her body washed up on shore."

Lily listened intently, feeling an aching sadness in her heart for poor Ana. She couldn't help but think of Kara and how she had disappeared in a similar way so many years ago. It seemed like a cruel coincidence that both girls had vanished in such a mysterious manner. The main difference was, though, that Ana had been found… but Kara hadn't. Was that why no connection was ever drawn?

Lily could theorize on that all day, but Ana wasn't the main reason she wanted to see Astrid and Vivian.

"Girls," Lily said, taking one of the occult books out of her bag, "have you seen this before?"

Lily set it down on the table.

Astrid and Vivian's eyes widened in shock. The book was old and tattered, with a leather binding that had been stitched together with thick thread. The cover was adorned with strange symbols that Lily had never seen before, while the pages were filled with strange writings and illustrations. It was clear to them all that this was an occult book—one of those dark tomes that were whispered about in hushed tones, never spoken of aloud.

Astrid and Vivian looked at each other, a mixture of fear and curiosity mixed in their expressions.

Lily could see their eyes widen as they realized what it was they were looking at.

"Where did you get this?" Astrid asked, her voice barely above a whisper.

"I found it in Kara's room," Lily said quietly. "She never told me about it. I didn't know she liked things like this. Did she?"

Astrid and Vivian exchanged a concerned look. "Well…"

Lily pressed them, sensing they knew more than they were letting on. "Please, tell me what you know. I need to find out the truth about her disappearance."

The girls hesitated, looking at each other nervously. Finally, Vivian spoke up.

"Kara had been fascinated by the occult for a while," she said slowly. "We had all heard stories about it and were curious, but Kara was really into it. She would stay up late reading books like that one and researching different rituals and spells online."

Astrid nodded in agreement. "She kept saying she wanted to do something big… she called it 'a great work.' We weren't sure what it meant exactly but we knew that it was something important to her."

Lily felt a chill run down her spine as Astrid and Vivian recounted the details of Kara's fascination with the occult. It seemed like she had been searching for something—something she must have thought would help her with whatever goal or dream she was chasing after so desperately. But what could it have been?

"Anyway, it was her idea to go see…" Astrid trailed off.

Lily frowned. "Go see what?"

"Are we really gonna tell her about that?" Vivian mumbled. "It was so crazy and weird…"

"What was?" Lily's heart picked up.

Vivian sighed. "Look, it was Kara's idea, but when we were kids, probably a few months before Kara disappeared, we went to go see this weird lady on one of the surrounding islands."

"What 'weird lady'?" Lily asked, frowning. "Neither of you ever thought it was relevant to tell this to the police?"

"Well, no!" Vivian exclaimed.

"She was a witch," Astrid cut in. "The whole thing was just weird. It definitely had nothing to do with what happened to Kara—or Ana."

"Tell me what happened," Lily said. She was no longer here just as Kara's sister, but an FBI agent too. This could be key information, information that should've been given a lot sooner.

"Well," Vivian started, "when we arrived, the witch told us that if we each put a drop of our blood on the pages of her book, and made a wish for our future, she would grant us all life-long romances. We thought it was silly and ridiculous, so none of us really took it seriously."

Astrid nodded in agreement. "I mean, why wouldn't we do it? It was just a silly thing kids do when they're bored and looking for something to do. We didn't think anything of it."

"But what about Kara?" Lily pressed. "Did she believe in it?"

"I mean, yeah, kinda," Astrid said. "You probably didn't know this, but Kara always wanted a boyfriend. She was kind of jealous that you seemed to get so much attention."

"What?" Lily's heart plummeted. Did her sister really feel that way? That didn't line up with her memory of quiet, studious Kara.

"Sorry," Vivian said. "It's true, though."

"Tell me more about the witch," Lily said, keeping on topic.

"Well," Astrid continued, "when we were leaving, Kara stopped and told the witch that she was searching for something else. The witch said she could help her if Kara was willing to pay a price. We never found out what it was."

Lily's mind raced. Was the old witch the key to finding out what happened to her sister? Could this be the lead they had been searching for all these years? It seemed so strange, and yet it was the most Lily had to go on.

She had to investigate further. If there was a chance that this witch could provide any information on Kara's disappearance, then Lily would do whatever it took to find her. She had to know the truth, and she knew that this might be her only chance. Whatever the truth may be, one thing was certain: Lily needed to find out more about the witch and her connection to the occult if she ever wanted to discover the answers she so desperately sought.

She knew there was only so much Astrid and Vivian could tell her. If Lily truly wanted answers, then she had to get her hands on this.

This apparent old witch—she could answer all of Lily's questions.

She leaned forward intensely. "Tell me where I can find her."

<u>STILL HERE</u>
(A Lily Dawn FBI Suspense Thriller —Book 4)

FBI BAU Special Agent Lily Dawn, half Dutch, half Hispanic, raised in the Caribbean, knows the isles like the back of her hand. When a surge in serial killers in the region prods the FBI to assemble a task force, Lily is the natural choice. But Lily is reluctant to face the demons of her past, including her missing sister, and when a serial killer leaves a trail of victims in marinas, Lily must race to enter the killer's mind and decode the riddle. Who will he claim next?

"The plot has many twists and turns, but it is the ending, which I did not see coming at all, that totally defines this book as one of the most riveting that I have read in years."
—Reader review for Not Like Us

STILL HERE is book #4 in a long-anticipated new series by #1 bestseller Ava Strong, whose bestseller NOT LIKE US (a free download) has received over 1,000 five star ratings and reviews.

A complex psychological crime thriller full of twists and turns and packed with heart-pounding suspense, the LILY DAWN mystery series will make you fall in love with a brilliant new female protagonist and keep you turning pages late into the night.

Future books in the series are now also available.

"This is a chilling, suspenseful page turner that just might leave you scared at night!"
—Reader review for Not Like Us

"Very intriguing, kept me turning page after page… Lots of twists and turns and a very unexpected ending. Cannot wait for the next in this series!"
—Reader review for Not Like Us

"A roller coaster ride of events… Can't put down until you finish it!"

—Reader review for Not Like Us

“Excellent read with very realistic characters that you become emotionally invested in… Couldn't put it down!”
—Reader review for The Death Code

“An excellent read, lots of twists and turns, with a surprising ending, leaving you wanting to read the next book in the series! Well done!”
—Reader review for The Death Code

“Well worth the read. Cannot wait to see what happens in the next book!”
—Reader review for The Death Code

“Quickly became a story I couldn’t put down! I highly recommend this book!”
—Reader review for His Other Wife

“I really enjoyed the fast-paced action, plot design and characterization... I didn't want to put the book down and the ending was a total surprise.”
—Reader review for His Other Wife

“The characters are extremely well developed… There are twists and turns in the plot that kept me guessing. An extremely well written story.”
—Reader review for His Other Wife

Ava Strong

Ava Strong is author of the REMI LAURENT mystery series, comprising six books (and counting); of the ILSE BECK mystery series, comprising seven books (and counting); of the STELLA FALL psychological suspense thriller series, comprising six books (and counting); of the DAKOTA STEELE FBI suspense thriller series, comprising six books (and counting); and of the LILY DAWN suspense thriller series, comprising five books (and counting).

An avid reader and lifelong fan of the mystery and thriller genres, Ava loves to hear from you, so please feel free to visit www.avastrongauthor.com to learn more and stay in touch.

BOOKS BY AVA STRONG

LILY DAWN FBI SUSPENSE THRILLER
STILL ALIVE (Book #1)
STILL HOPE (Book #2)
STILL AWAKE (Book #3)
STILL HERE (Book #4)
STILL MAD (Book #5)

REMI LAURENT FBI SUSPENSE THRILLER
THE DEATH CODE (Book #1)
THE MURDER CODE (Book #2)
THE MALICE CODE (Book #3)
THE VENGEANCE CODE (Book #4)
THE DECEPTION CODE (Book #5)
THE SEDUCTION CODE (Book #6)

ILSE BECK FBI SUSPENSE THRILLER
NOT LIKE US (Book #1)
NOT LIKE HE SEEMED (Book #2)
NOT LIKE YESTERDAY (Book #3)
NOT LIKE THIS (Book #4)
NOT LIKE SHE THOUGHT (Book #5)
NOT LIKE BEFORE (Book #6)
NOT LIKE NORMAL (Book #7)

STELLA FALL PSYCHOLOGICAL SUSPENSE THRILLER
HIS OTHER WIFE (Book #1)
HIS OTHER LIE (Book #2)
HIS OTHER SECRET (Book #3)
HIS OTHER MISTRESS (Book #4)
HIS OTHER LIFE (Book #5)
HIS OTHER TRUTH (Book #6)

DAKOTA STEELE FBI SUSPENSE THRILLER
WITHOUT MERCY (Book #1)
WITHOUT REMORSE (Book #2)
WITHOUT A PAST (Book #3)
WITHOUT PITY (Book #4)
WITHOUT HOPE (Book #5)

Made in United States
North Haven, CT
17 October 2023

42867242R10086